It's another triumph of dumb luck over talent as
Pat Riordan solves a murder more or less by
remote control. Riordan and the ever-loyal Reiko,
his indomitable partner, are sent off to South
Florida to find a client's elderly aunt, but when
they find the lady she has been dispatched in a
most execrable fashion. However, the pair returns
to the Monterey Peninsula of California and all
the threads end in a Carmel restaurant on a
bright, sunshiny day.

# Just Another
# Murder in Miami

Other books by this author:

Roy Gilligan

# Just Another Murder in Miami

Brendan Books
CARMEL, CALIFORNIA

Art direction by Robin Gilligan
Cover art by Reed Farrington
Photography by SplashStudios
Book design and typography by Jim Cook/Santa Barbara

Copyright ©1994 by Roy Gilligan
Published by
   Brendan Books
   P.O. Box 221143
   Carmel, California 93922

Manufactured in the United States of America.

1-94

Library of Congress Catalog Card Number 93-73507
ISBN 0-9626136-5-7

*This one is for the World's Greatest Cartoonist (retired)
and his beautiful wife*

## GUS & FRANCES ARRIOLA

*without whose friendship and encouragement,
the Pat Riordan series would never have got off the ground.*

It should be quite clear that this is a work of fiction, all except the scene in Miami where Reiko gets her purse snatched in the rental car. This actually happened to the author and his long-suffering spouse.

I'm especially indebted to Walter Georis, artist, vintner, restaurateur par excellence, for allowing me to deprive him of his two active young sons and their mother so that he could pose for the character of Armand. There *is* a restaurant called Casanova, a very good one, indeed. And there's one called the General Store, too, just up the street. So much for reality.

I must thank my good friend Reed Farrington for another colorful cover painting. It's a grabber. And a low bow to Will Smith, brave soul of an editor, for pointing out the glitches in the manuscript. And much love to Jane, my wife, and Robin, my daughter, for all the support they have given me over the years.

# Just Another
# Murder in Miami

# 1
## "Armand, I don't go to Miami."

WHEN I knocked on Armand's door that morning, I really didn't know what to expect. He had called me the night before, in a sort of panic, summoning me to his house in hushed and mysterious tones to discuss something of "vital importance."

Now, I knew that over the years the only thing of really "vital importance" to Armand was the bottom line. How much the restaurant made, how many bottles of wine were sold, how much profit. So I wasn't too excited. The guy has caught one of his trusted employees stealing, I thought after his call. I hope it wasn't one of his relatives. He wants me to bus dishes for him so that I can sneak up on the culprit. But all of his people know me. That couldn't be it.

I didn't hear any sound in the house after my first knock, so I knocked again, pretty hard. Still nothing. I waited about thirty seconds and then pounded the door with my fist, yelling "Armand, dammit, I know you're in there."

Soft sounds, maybe like bare feet on plush carpet, came from within. The door opened slightly. Armand's large brown eyes looked at me through a six-inch space. I tried to push through, but he held the door tightly against me.

"I'm sorry, Pat. I heard you the first time. I was awake. The trouble is—well, it really isn't trouble—I can't find my pants. I know I took them off last night. But this morning I can't find them. You know how it is."

"I do *not* know how it is, Armand. There have been times when I have misplaced my wallet or lost my keys. But I have always found my pants. Where the hell did you leave them?"

The door opened a little wider and I was able to slip through. He was standing before me, clean-shaven and impeccably groomed, but with no pants. I was surprised to note that his legs, which I had never seen before, were rather thin and knobby, and his toenails were badly in need of a trim. But he was wearing boxers and he looked for all the world like a bewildered Carmel summer tourist who had just discovered that the ocean breezes can really affect a man's virility when they sneak up his floppy shorts.

"Come in, come in," he said. He did not look at me directly, searching the room, it seemed, for the missing pants.

I tried to sympathize. "Armand, you must have other pants. Why don't you just put a pair on and let it go at that. The lost ones will show up."

"It isn't that," he said. "Jennifer was here last evening, and—well, things got a bit passionate. I flung caution to the winds . . . and I must have flung my pants with it. It's just not like me."

True. Armand is usually completely in charge. Nothing escapes his eagle eye in the restaurant. He personally supervises the filling of each bottle at the winery. But that morning he was completely unstrung because he couldn't find his pants.

"Sit down, Pat, please." He collapsed onto a sofa, half sitting, half reclining. I took a chair across the room.

10

He had regained his composure to a degree. He finally looked directly at me. "Pat, you have known me quite a long while. You know that I am not easily disturbed. And you know how close-knit my family is." He hid his face in his hands for a long moment and let me sit there twiddling my thunbs.

"So, go ahead, Armand. What's buggin' you? Woman trouble? Embezzlement? Hemorrhoids? What?"

He sat up straight on the couch. "You know of my treasured aunt in Miami?"

"No, Armand. I have never heard of an aunt in Florida. I thought your whole damn' family was here." I was getting a little irritated.

"She is my favorite, Pat. She has been living there alone for many years. I have made it a habit to call her at least once a month for years. Just to make sure she was all right, you understand. However, during the past week, I have called her frequently, but her phone does not answer. I am afraid of foul play. She has often gone off on trips to Europe or Asia or South America, but she has always kept me informed of her travels."

"Doesn't she have any friends? Can't you get in touch with somebody who knows about her?"

"She has been something of a recluse. I do not know the names of any of her acquaintances. I am stumped, Riordan."

"So, what do you want me to do? Call the Miami cops? Enter a missing persons report? Goddamit, Armand, what can I do from here?"

He took a deep breath. "I want you to go to Miami and find my aunt. Or, at least, discover what has happened to her. I, of course, will pay all your expenses, plus a reasonable fee."

That shook me up a bit. "Reasonable fee" shook me up. Armand was very cagey with a buck. But what really shocked me was his request that I go to Miami.

"Armand, I don't go to Miami. I seldom leave California. I'm licensed as a private investigator *only* in California. Now, maybe if I got in touch with Travis McGee, but he's not really a PI. . . ."

"Don't jest with me, Pat. This is a serious matter. And you're the only investigator I know." He rose from the couch and walked to a desk in the corner of the room. From a drawer, he extracted a huge check book, one of those deals with three or four checks to a page.

"How much do you require as an advance? Two thousand, three thousand, five thousand?"

"Armand, I'm trying to tell you that I just don't *go* to Florida. I have no authority there. I have little enough *here*. Reiko couldn't handle things without me." I knew that last was an out-and-out lie. Reiko could very well handle things without me. Maybe she might even prefer to do without me for a while.

"Take her with you. You see, Riordan, my aunt is very important to me. I will spare no expense."

There wasn't very much I could do. Business hadn't been all that overwhelming on the Monterey Peninsula. We were in a fairly dry period. Maybe, just maybe, it wouldn't be so bad. Maybe it'd be fun.

"I'll have to ask Reiko, Armand. She's my partner, you know. She's got to approve or disapprove. But I'll ask. When do you need to know?"

"Yesterday, Riordan. Here's your check. Five thousand dollars. Of course, I want every bit accounted for."

"You hold it for now, Armand. I . . . I really don't know if this thing will fly."

"It will fly." He tucked the check into my shirt pocket. "I want you on your way tomorrow."

Armand can be a very forceful guy, even without his pants. When he made up his mind about something, it was like cast in bronze.

I left the house a little dazed. It was perfectly true that I hadn't been away from the West Coast for quite a stretch. Some of my California cases had led me to connections in

Washington, Oregon and Nevada. But I had not been east of Reno for I don't know how many years.

Driving from Armand's house on Casanova in Carmel to my office on Alvarado Street in Monterey, I began to feel better about the mission upon which I was probably about to embark. But what about Reiko? And what about Sally? Sally is the lady of my choice, a Carmel travel agent who warms my heart and my bed, but will not marry me. How will she feel about my flying off to the East?

I shook off all my doubts as I hit the top of Carmel hill and took the Munras off-ramp into Monterey. But at that time, I really didn't know what was in store for me. That trip to Miami brought me more grief than I ever anticipated. Any guy who would name his restaurant after the street he lived on has got to be just a little eccentric. If I had known—even suspected—what was going to happen, I would have told Armand to stick his five thousand bucks up where the sun don't shine.

## 2
# *"You're going to Miami with Reiko?"*

"**I** DON'T KNOW," said Reiko. "I've got no family there. I just don't like to go anywhere I haven't got a cousin or two. And who was it who said, 'Florida is wonderful . . . if you're an orange.'"

She was slouching against the door frame of what I like to call my private office, making small circles with her right foot on the bare floor.

"I think it was Fred Allen, but you wouldn't remember him. Honey, it isn't as if we're going to *stay* there. It'll take a week. Ten days at the most. Armand's paying the bills. We could maybe run up to Disney World. Hey, call it a mini-vaca-tion."

She walked slowly over to my desk, planted her hands on it and leaned forward with narrowed eyes.

"You and *me*? Off to the other side of the country together? What will Sally think?"

"She'll understand," I said, but I wasn't really sure about

14

that. Although Reiko and I have never been involved in what you might call a love affair, Sally knows I have a weakness for my tiny sansei partner, and she might think—Oh, what the hell.

Reiko sensed my thoughts. "A long time ago you proposed to me, remember? You had never laid a hand on me, and you haven't since. But you proposed. In what I assume was a moment of weakness and terrible loneliness. Just after I came to work for you. But do you really think Sally Morse will just sort of ignore our dashing off together . . . in an airplane . . . to a far off hotel in a semi-tropical sort of resort place?"

"Well, she just damn well better!" I had made up my mind. I didn't quite know how I was going to break it to Sally, but she'd just have to accept that Reiko and I were professional associates and going off on a case together.

Reiko shrugged. "Okay by me. When do we leave? You gonna have Sal make the arrangements?"

Oh, God, I thought, Sally *is* in the travel business. She'd just naturally expect to handle the details for a long and somewhat complicated trip. Besides, there was the matter of a commission. Reiko did a little ballet turn and walked back to her desk outside the partition. I called Sally.

"You're *what*? Going to Miami with Reiko? I hope you've got a good story for this one, pal."

I explained as best I could. Armand was a friend, an old friend. I was sort of obligated to make an effort to find his aunt. And he was paying all the expenses. Sally seemed to calm down a bit. She seemed resigned and weary as she shifted into her business mode and asked the usual questions.

"When do you want to go? You know you can't get there from here. You can fly direct from L.A., if you want to take one of the commuter trips to the south. *Or* you can take American out of San Jose, but you'll have to go through Dallas-Ft. Worth or maybe O'Hare in Chicago. You can take Delta, but you'll have to change in Atlanta. And what kind of accomodations do you want?" Her voice took on a hard edge. "Two *single* rooms, of course."

15

"Any way that's the quickest, Sal. And a hotel in northeast Miami. The way I get it, the town is all divided into quarters, and Armand's aunt's place is in a little enclave called Miami Shores. And we've got to go soonest."

"Do you realize that today is Thursday and tomorrow is Friday?"

"So I've got a calendar, honey."

"And it's the beginning of Easter Week. You know Easter is early this year."

I still didn't get it. "So?"

"Riordan, getting you seats on an airline is going to be difficult, to say the least. And without advance reservations, you're going to have to pay the full scheduled round-trip fare. Are you—is Armand prepared for that?"

"How much money's involved?"

"A hell of a lot. You know how the airlines are. When the traffic is heavy they raise the fares to make up for the slack seasons. Unless you make reservations weeks ahead, you go full fare. How does that strike you?"

"Send the bill to Armand. Get us out of here tomorrow, if you can. Do whatever it takes. And Sal . . ."

"Yes?"

"Don't worry. I'm not gonna play grabass with Reiko. Honest I'm not."

"I'll call you back in an hour," she said, rather coldly.

I leaned back in my chair and clasped my hands behind my head. I had been to Miami once, long ago. My father decided to take his vacation in December and figured that Florida, with its palm trees and flamingos, would be a better place to go than Stinson Beach, north of San Francisco. And it would be educational for me.

All I could remember from that trip was a motel on a strip of land north of Miami Beach called Sunny Isles. You walked down a steep flight of wooden stairs to the beach, which was about four feet wide at that point. I nearly got stung by a Portuguese man-of-war and watched the lifeguard beat the thing to a pulp with a baseball bat. And it was really cold in sunny, tropical Florida that winter.

Maybe this trip would be much more pleasant. And maybe not. But I didn't expect the total weirdness that I got.

## 3
## *"We have one room with twin beds."*

I'M NOT really sure that Sally put forth a lot of effort on behalf of Reiko and me, but when she called back she told me that the best she could get for us was a flight on American out of San Jose.

"You'll have to get off at Dallas-Ft. Worth, but you get right back on the same plane. It's not a through flight exactly, but it's the best I could do. Your rooms are at Howard Johnson's on Biscayne Boulevard. But you'll get to Miami after midnight, so I booked you just overnight at one of the places near the airport. I reserved a rental car for you, so you can go on up to HoJo's the next morning."

"Thanks, Sal. When do we leave?"

"Tomorrow. One o'clock. Flight 153 out of San Jose Airport. You've got to make your own arrangements to get there. Bon voyage."

I felt a little guilty.

"Sally, you *do* understand, don't you? I've *got* to go. And

18

Reiko will be a great deal of help to me. We'll only be gone a week or ten days. We'll. . . . "

"Save it, Riordan. I know you'll behave. You're a Korean War veteran, right? All you guys have to be of a certain age. You know, when most of the wax in the wick has melted. You're no stud, lover. I know, better than anybody else. Have a good time." She hung up.

That hurt. I mean, she could have been nicer. But, on the other hand, she was just a bit jealous. She loves me, I thought. Why the hell won't she marry me when I ask her?

The next morning Reiko and I took off for San Jose. She insisted on driving. "That'll cut fifteen or twenty minutes off the trip, Riordan. I've got a heavier foot."

I knew that. Riding with Reiko is a memorable experience. When it's my car she always complains about the automatic transmission. "Wimps drive these things, Riordan," she says. She turns the radio on full volume to some top-forty rock station, glues her eyes on the road and her hands in the ten and two position on the wheel. She does not speak, she does not listen. It's like being catapulted out of a slingshot in a cacaphony of rock music along Highway 101.

We got to the airport in plenty of time for a quick lunch. The plane was loaded faster than I could hope, and we flew off into the mysterious East.

After you've lived in California as long as I have, *everything* about the East is mysterious. We're a curious lot, Californians. Those of us who were born and raised here anyhow. Not many of us are much interested in traveling to the east coast. We think we've got it all. We never think about earthquakes or droughts . . . until they happen.

Reiko settled in her seat in the 757 and tugged at her seat belt.

"When's he gonna hit the light? We've been up for ten minutes and he ought to hit the light. I don't like to be tied down."

I knew that. She gets very fidgety when she has to stay in

the same place very long. And we were in for about five and a half hours for the trip, including the stop in Dallas-Ft. Worth.

But we made it without incident. Well, almost without incident. Coming into Miami we ran through a thunderstorm and the lightning was flashing all around us. I had almost forgotten about thunderstorms. We get so few of 'em on the Monterey Peninsula. But the plane landed safely and I released my death-grip on the armrest.

I will not go into the details of how we arrived, dressed far too warmly for a hot, humid semi-tropical night. The airport seemed to be undergoing some renovation, and the walk to the baggage claim area was much too long. Let's just say we got our stuff and got out. A minibus took us to the car rental place, and we got directions to the hotel.

"Riordan," I said to the clerk. "We've got reservations."

"Yes?"

"Yes. Riordan. Two singles. Look, man, we just got off a plane from California, and we're bushed."

"Yes, of course. I am truly very sorry, Mr. Riordan, but we have not two single rooms left. You are arriving very late, you understand. We have *one* room with twin beds." He managed a smile and a shrug. "Best we can do."

"Give me the key." I glanced at Reiko, who was glaring at the room clerk with murder in her eyes. "We'll take what you've got. Can somebody bring up our bags?"

The clerk managed to summon a very old bellhop who spoke little or no English to carry our bags to the room. Reiko was whispering little obscenities to herself.

In the room, after I had dismissed the ancient bellhop with too big a tip, she turned on me.

"Sally did this! She screwed up the reservation. I know she doesn't like me, but this is too much."

"Hold it, little one. Sally wouldn't have dared do this. It's the hotel's fault. We've just got to make the best of it."

She calmed down after a few minutes, but she never stopped muttering to herself. I don't think she said a word to me the rest of the night. She just disappeared into the bathroom, washed her face, put on her pajamas and emerged to crawl into bed. In a short time, I could tell by her regular breathing that she was asleep.

Y'know, it's funny. Here I was in a hotel room with a much younger woman, and I didn't even think of trying to seduce her. Am I really that old? Or just tired? Or do I love Sally too much? I was still asking myself unanswerable questions when I went to sleep.

Very early the next morning, we both woke up. Reiko woke first. She was sitting up when I looked over at her.

"Look at these pillows in the daylight, Riordan. This one looks like somebody threw up on it. What kind of a place is this, anyhow?"

"It's a fleabag, honey, but we're out of here right now."
And we were, just as fast as we could move.

# 4
## *The kid grabbed Reiko's purse and ran like hell.*

$A$T THIS POINT it wouldn't be right to try to explain to you the relationship of Armand's Aunt Therese and Herman Applegate, because at this point I didn't know anything about it. Therese Colbert, Armand's father's oldest sister, had never married. When the family had come from Belgium to America, the Colberts had fled across the country to California, having been overwhelmed by the noisy Manhattan neighborhood in which they first settled.

All except Therese. A particularly good-looking girl, she parlayed an inheritance of a few thousand dollars into a career in show business. Therese was a gypsy. That's what they call 'em in the show business. She was a dancer who sang a little, or a singer who danced quite well. She was much in demand because of her beauty and her dancing, but her really special talent was for attracting male admirers who spent fortunes on her, making it possible for the lady to invest all her cash in blue chip stocks which never went anywhere but up.

Therese, like all the Colberts, had high principles. She would never have thought of actually *marrying* a man for his money, with divorce and a rich settlement in mind. But swain after swain kept her in luxury until middle-age began to set in and the propositions she had entertained for many years became fewer and farther between, and they came from increasingly older, less affluent men.

But, by this time, Therese was financially independent and had enjoyed all the romance she needed over a productive life-time. She bought a modest little house in what was then the quaint village of Miami Shores on the north edge of Miami proper, which has, in the course of time, been surrounded by prodigious real estate developments. Her ambition had been, from earliest childhood, to visit every country in the world, and that is what she set out to do.

Until she met Herman Applegate. Herman worked for the Soul of Discretion Escort Bureau in North Miami Beach, and Therese had availed herself of his services on many occasions, particularly in the seventies and eighties, when the ardor of voluntary lovers had ebbed. But Herman was not much of a person

However, I didn't find that out right away.

After that miserable night in the nameless hotel at the Miami Airport, I made bold to ask the daytime desk clerk for directions to Miami Shores.

"Where?" he asked.

"Miami Shores. I'v got an address here on 92nd street."

"Northeast or northwest?"

"Northwest."

"OK, you go outta here on LeJeune—that's LeJeune out there, got it?—well, it turns inta 8th Avenue goin' north. Y'turn right at, maybe, about 25th Street which'll turn inta about 79th Street, an' ya follow it to Miami Avenue where you turn left, headin' north. Then ask somebody."

I had painstakingly written down the man's careful instructions. With a sinking feeling, I thanked him and escorted

Reiko out to our rented automobile. A small, sweating bell-hop, who looked as though he should be riding at Hialeah, struggled behind with our bags.

Rental cars are a pain in the ass. Oh, they're always pretty new, and in good shape. But they're never anything like cars I'm used to driving. I have to fumble around for the ignition switch, search for the wiper control, experiment with the lights and, as often as not, fight with the automatic restraining belt that creepily snugs up to my chest when I start the car. Thank God most of 'em have the gear levers and brake pedals in similar positions.

Off we went, heading north. After a couple of miles of eas-ily forgettable drab blocks, I felt uneasy. Trying to drive an unfamiliar car and catch the street signs as I passed without going through a red light or knocking down a pedestrian was getting to me. "I think we're lost," I said to Reiko.

"Just great, Riordan. You told me you'd been in this town before."

"When I was eight, love, when I was eight. It just ain't the same place. Here, let's pull over and take a look at the map."

I turned right at the next important-looking intersection, and left on the first side street. We dragged out the Miami city map and held it against the dash. I had just put my finger on our destination (which wasn't all that far away) when the door on Reiko's side flew open and a very large young man pushed her violently against me and grabbed her purse.

It happened so fast. The kid grabbed Reiko's purse and ran like hell. I recovered in seconds, but all I could think to do was follow the sonofabitch in the car. What I would have done if I had caught up with him, I have no idea. He cut back against me and I jumped out of the car and pursued him on foot.

Now, this guy was maybe six-two, 220, like nineteen years old, and here I was wheezing after him with murder in my heart. He went over a six-foot cyclone fence into a residential yard, and disappeared. I clung to the fence, out of breath.

"Welcome to Miami," I thought. Reiko brought the car up alongside me.

"What the hell did you think you were doing, chasing that kid? He coulda had a knife or a gun. He outweighed you by fifty pounds."

I was breathing hard. "Flag somebody down. Call the cops. Or just go away and let me die." I managed to sit down on the curb.

She was off like a shot and miraculously returned in less than a minute with a thin, gray-haired black man who pointed us in the direction of the nearest police station.

Suffice it to say that the Metro-Dade police were polite and efficient, but that they were pretty much of the opinion that Reiko would never see that purse again, or anything that was in it.

"Shit!" she said, when they told her that. "Drivers license, credit cards, ID, *everything*. Hey, I've never been a crime victim before. And I sure as hell didn't fly all the way across the country to be initiated."

Welcome to Miami.

# 5

# *It was the unmistakable stink of decay.*

WE GOT a police escort to Therese's little house in Miami Shores. Not that we needed it, you understand. When I got my wind back I was furious, with the kid who swiped the purse *and* myself.

"Maybe Balestreri's right. Maybe Greg is right. Maybe I should carry a piece. If I'd had a gun, I could have dropped that bastard in his tracks before he got twenty feet away. Sonofabitch!"

Tony Balestreri of the Monterey County Sheriff's Office and Greg Farrell, a free-wheeling artist and Reiko's sometime boyfriend, had urged me to arm myself if I was going to remain in the private detective business.

"Look, Mighty Mouse, if you had plugged the kid and he was unarmed, you could go to jail for a long time. Self-defense which results in homicide is only justified if the threat is as lethal as the reaction. You taught me that yourself."

Reiko is remarkably cool, under any and all circumstances. I guessed that she had already made plans to replace her ID and cancel her credit cards.

Maybe I should explain that I hate guns. Despite all those hard rock fictional PI's, there are a few of us around. I am of a certain age (as Sally said) and fought as an infantry private in Korea. Any illusions I had as a youth about guns ("Bang, bang, you're dead, Kevin.") were very quickly dispelled when I heard bullets whine by, and saw friends die in a most unnecessary way. When the army turned me loose, I swore never to own a firearm. Screw the NRA. Guns don't give you extra balls.

But then I had never thought of becoming a private investigator. I sort of fell into the profession by accident, but that's another story. It involves my legal education and a lot of Scotch with only a splash of water.

Eventually the cop car pulled up in front of the address that Armand had given me for his aunt. The officer who was driving got out of his car and walked up to us. "This the address? I'm not sure about this neighborhood, Mr. Riordan. That place across the street. I think that's the one that used to be a crack house. There was a report on it a few months back."

I looked at the address I had scribbled on a piece of paper at Armand's house. "This is it, officer. I'm sure. Thanks for your escort."

The policeman squinted at the house. "Looks empty. You sure you don't want us to hang around?"

"No, thanks. You've helped a lot. We'll take it from here." If there was no response at the door, I knew we might have to do a little breaking and entering, and I didn't want the cops for witnesses.

"Okay," he said. But he gave us a slightly suspicious look as he drove off.

After sitting for a few minutes to evaluate the territory, Reiko and I got out of the car and approached the house.

I rang the doorbell and waited. It was a small place and I

could hear the chimes clearly from the outside. No way some-body inside could have missed the sound, unless the person were deaf. There was no response. I knocked on the door. After a moment, I knocked again. Nothing.

"Try the door," said Reiko.

I grabbed the knob and turned it easily. "It's not locked. Goddamit, an old lady lives alone across from a crack house and doesn't lock her door. Gotta be senile. Gotta be out of it."

The door swung open into the living room of the house. A ceiling fan spun slowly, with little effect. The fan pushed the stale, humid air around, but didn't do much else. "That thing is turned on," I said to no one in particular, although Reiko was standing beside me. "Why is it turned on if there's nobody home?"

To our right was an arch which led to a short hallway con-necting two tiny bedrooms with a small bathroom. All were empty. There was a very particular odor in the room, one that I had smelled before. At the far end of the living room, to the left was the kitchen, an indescribable mess. The sink was full of dirty dishes. A toaster oven looked as if it had been used over and over again without cleaning. The oven in the stove was full of bags of crackers and potato chips.

"She sure doesn't eat at home much." Reiko pulled out a bag of potato chips and tasted one. "Stale. Ugh. God, I hope she doesn't eat *these* things."

There was one room left, a sort of solarium with jalousied windows folks in these parts call a Florida room. It was sepa-rated by a door at the end of the living room.

The door was ajar, and I pushed it open.

The odor I had recognized when we arrived was intense in the Florida room. It was the unmistakable stink of decay. My eyes were immediately drawn to a pair of stockinged feet extending from behind a wicker settee. In a crazy moment I flashed to the scene in *The Wizard of Oz* where Dorothy pulls off the ruby slippers of the Wicked Witch of the East, and the feet roll up like one of those party noisemakers. I pulled the dusty piece of furniture away, and there was Aunt Therese, lying on her back with dried blood all over her chest. She'd been there a while, and her body had begun to decompose. Reiko came up from behind me. "Jesus!" was all she could say.

Well, we had found Armand's aunt for him. All I had to do was call him and tell him the old lady was dead and not to worry, right? But that would never do. Here we were, as far as we could get from home and still stay in the U.S. of A. And we had a murder on our hands.

# 6

# *"It sure as hell isn't a scorpion sting."*

M<small>Y</small> STOMACH was used to death. I mean I don't get nauseated at the sight of a dead body. There were too many of them in Korea, ours and theirs. Bodies in awkward, unnatural positions, with parts missing or smashed to a pulp. The smell was there, too, overwhelming everything else: the acrid stink of gunpowder, the trenches outside Korean villages where they dumped all their human waste to be saved for fertilizer. And here we were in sunny Florida.

I pulled my gaze away from the body of Therese Colbert and looked through the jalousied windows into the backyard of her home. "What's that tree?" I asked Reiko.

She had turned her back to the grisly scene and reluctantly took a peek. "That's an orange tree, stupid. In case you don't know it, we've got 'em in California."

"Why aren't there any oranges on it?" I asked in all innocence.

"The season's over. Don't you know anything, Riordan?"

We were both pretty shaken. I turned to Reiko and we went back into the living room. I closed the door tightly behind us.

"Okay, partner, what do we do now?" Reiko's color was not good. Let me state for once and all that Japanese people are not "yellow" any more than Indians are "red".

Reiko's complexion changes with her moods even as my own pale Irish skin does. She's not given to the display of anger or sadness in her face, but her color often gives her away.

"Let's sit down." I nudged her to a rumpled couch that was in obvious need of cleaning.

"I think," I began, "that it is necessary to call the police. What do you think we ought to tell them?"

"Don't ask me. You're the senior partner."

I was not eager to approach Therese Colbert's body again, but I knew I had to. "I'll go back in there and take a closer look. Maybe I can find out something about how she died. You know, whether it was a bullet or a knife or something else."

"Something else? My God, Riordan, what else could it be. It sure as hell isn't a scorpion sting." Reiko's color was improving and her feistiness was returning.

I went back into the Florida room, pulled away the wicker settee and knelt by the body. Leaning close to the corpse and trying not to breathe, I concluded that the woman had been stabbed. The wound in her chest appeared, to the unaided eye, to be a knife slash rather than a bullet wound, but it was hard to tell. I figured it had been delivered on the spot and she fell where she was attacked. There seemed to be no evidence that the body had been dragged from some other place. It might have been that she had got behind the settee to avoid attack, but was overpowered. That was about as far as I could go. I didn't want to touch the body before the coroner arrived.

"Okay," I said, again closing the door against the awful stench of death, "let's call the cops."

31

I found the phone on a small writing desk and dialed 911. I gave my name and the address to the operator and told her that there was a dead body on the premises. I told her I was an investigator from California and that I would wait for the police in the house. I'm not sure that she believed me, but she took the information and told me there would be somebody at the house in a matter of minutes.

"Well, kid, we've both been shot in the line of duty. Now we've discovered a murder victim together. Does this mean we're soul mates?"

"You're fulla shit, Riordan. God, doesn't a dead body upset you at all?"

I didn't tell her it didn't, because it did. But, as I said already, it wasn't anything new to an old foot soldier. I just absorbed the upset and went on living, as I had done many times before.

I was at that moment caught up in a small sweet memory of a time when my father lifted me up to an orange tree to let me pick a ripe fruit. It was in an orange grove in Southern California in the thirties, when there were still orange groves close to Los Angeles. The whole place smelled so sweet. Death among the oranges. Doesn't sound right.

At that moment I heard the police car roll up and come to a noisy stop outside the front door.

# 7
## "*Ah, a* woman."

I HAD SOME heavy explaining to do when the cops arrived. Who was I? Why was I here? How did I get in the house?

Having had a little experience dealing with police investigations, I carefully laid out the details as I knew them. The lady, I told them, was an aunt of a client of mine in Carmel, California. He hadn't been able to get in touch with her for a couple of weeks. He was alarmed and apprehensive, so he sent me, a licensed California PI, to see if I could find her.

"I suppose you know, sir, that you're not supposed to operate professionally in Florida." The young policeman had a round pink face and just the hint of a mustache.

"I'm very well aware of it, officer. I came here as a favor to a friend who was distressed about his inability to get hold of a favorite relative. For reasons of his own, he didn't want to go through ordinary channels." What I meant was that Armand felt that the police might take him for a crank and ignore his concern for his missing aunt. But I couldn't say that. Actually the cops in the Miami area have their hands full twenty-four hours a day with a variety of problems.

After an hour of questioning, the officers let us go with the usual stern warning not to leave the area. I gave them the address of the Howard Johnson's on Biscayne and said they could find us there. Better composed but near exhaustion, Reiko and I climbed back into the rental car and rolled off to find the hotel.

It wasn't a bad place, but the air-conditioning was not the most efficient, and the food was typical HoJo's: inexpensive, filling, and undistinguished. The next couple of days passed slowly.

Reiko and I had adjoining rooms this time. We'd ride around town during the day and sit in my room and watch TV at night. She had lost no time cancelling her credit cards and calling the California DMV for a duplicate driver's license. But we both felt oppressed by the heat and humidity and the obligation to stagnate while waiting for the police to call.

On the third day, the phone rang in my room at eight o'clock in the morning.

"Mr. Riordan? Lieutenant Alvarez here. I am in charge of investigating the death of Miss Therese Colbert. Could I prevail upon you to meet me at Miss Colbert's house at ten this morning?" The voice was calm, with just a touch of Hispanic accent.

"Sure, Lieutenant. We'll be there."

"We? The officers who interrogated you did not speak of anyone else."

"My colleague was with me. I'm sure somebody talked to her."

"Ah, a *woman*. I see. Perhaps our people did not waste time with her."

Reiko didn't hear that, thank God. It was, perhaps, a proper Latino attitude, but it would have steamed her good. It irked *me* somewhat.

"Please don't say anything like that in my colleague's presence, Lieutenant Alvarez. She's a bit testy most of the time anyhow, and if she knows that she was written off in a murder case, there's no telling what she might do. She's small, you know, but she's a whiz at karate."

The lieutenant laughed heartily. I felt like telling the sonofabitch to keep it quiet. Reiko was in the next room and her hearing is excellent. I knew she was awake because the sound of her shower had awakened me at six-thirty.

"I will see you at ten o'clock, Mr. Riordan. Goodbye."

I lay back on the bed and closed my eyes. The bloody, shrunken body of the old lady in the cluttered little house was an indelible picture in my mind. I hadn't had the courage to call Armand at that point. It was necessary to find out more about Therese's life in Miami if I were to do anything about finding her killer. And the police investigation was hamstringing me.

"Okay, let's have breakfast, *rojin-san*." Reiko was standing over me, fully dressed, fresh as a daisy, ready to go. "What'll we do today? Can we ride up the beach and see the ocean? Remember, Armand's paying the bill."

I was wearing nothing but my jockey shorts, and I grabbed a blanket to cover my less-than-magnificent body.

"Why can't you knock? And lay off the *rojin* business. We've got to meet the cops at Therese's house at ten. Get out of here while I get dressed."

*Rojin* is one of Reiko's favorite Japanese words for me. Roughly, it means "old person with dignity." The "dignity" part is okay, but the "old" wounds me deeply.

Eventually, we left the hotel and drove back to the house on Northwest 92nd Street. Lieutenant Alvarez, a slender dark-haired man with a classic profile, met us at the door. He wore jeans and a neatly pressed short-sleeved white shirt.

"Thank you for coming. I think I have some illuminating news for you. Are you familiar with the name Herman Applegate?"

I'm sure I looked perfectly blank, because that's how I felt. The name meant nothing.

Alvarez went on: "We have been using Miss Colbert's address book to find her friends. Many of them mentioned Herman Applegate. The name means nothing to you?"

I shook my head. I glanced at Reiko. *She* didn't look a bit blank. As a matter of fact, she had that look of supreme confidence that she gets when she knows more than I do. She was faking it, however, because this time she didn't.

"Applegate, it seems, was a frequent caller here. A paid escort, I am told. Two of Miss Colbert's friends were most concerned about him. It appears that Miss Colbert had told them that she was planning to marry Mr. Applegate and go off with him to visit relatives in California. Her favorite nephew, she told them, was a prosperous businessman on the Monterey Peninsula, and she was looking forward to bringing home her first husband. Is it true? Had the lady never been married?"

"As far as I know." I was getting restless. So, what about Herman? I asked the officer: "Have you checked out Applegate?"

"Of course. He worked for an escort agency in Miami Beach. His employer tells us he resigned suddenly about ten days ago. Told them something about inheriting a large sum of money. Said he was moving to California."

That tore it. The killer of Therese Colbert had been traveling from east to west while Reiko and I were traveling west to east. We might have passed somewhere over Texas.

"Did Applegate kill Therese?" I asked. "Is there any hard evidence?"

"As a matter of fact, there is. A large knife. Carefully washed of blood, and put away in its proper drawer in the kitchen. Washed of blood, but not of fingerprints. The coroner has said that the size and shape of the wound indicate that the knife was most probably the murder weapon. The escort service was very helpful. They require police clearance of all their employees. His prints were on file. It's a match. Applegate is the killer."

It seemed like it was all over at that point. The woman was dead. The deadly weapon had been found. The murderer had been quickly identified by his having carelessly left his finger-prints on the deadly weapon. It was a wrap, right?

Wrong! Despite my temporary feeling of relief, the case was not over by a long shot. And there were miles to go before Reiko and I got a good night's sleep.

# 8

# Reiko and I packed in a hurry.

I CALLED Armand when we got back to the hotel.

"What do you know, Pat? Is she all right? Has she been ill?" He was anxious.

"Armand, old friend, the only way I know to break this to you is to put it up front. Therese Colbert is dead. We found her body. The cops here think that the deed was done by a gigolo-type named Herman Applegate. Therese had hired him through an escort service several times. A couple of her girl friends told the cops that Therese had told them she was going to marry the bastard. The cops told me that the guy is heading for California."

I could hear him taking slow deep breaths. He was very calm and deliberate when he spoke: "Thanks. How was she killed?"

"Stabbed. With a butcher knife, looks like. The knife was found in a drawer, washed clean. But it carried Applegate's finger prints. When he cleaned it, he just rinsed the fresh blood off, I guess. Didn't use any detergent. Greasy fingers left good prints."

Armand spoke very softly: "Herman Applegate is *here*, Pat. He is sitting at a front table in the restaurant, eating pasta. He arrived a few days ago, saying that he was my aunt's fiancé. He came, he said, to meet the rest of the family. Therese was to follow next week. What shall I do?"

"He's *there*? My God, don't do anything. Do an acting job, Armand. Try not to let him know that you know about Therese's murder. Just see that he doesn't leave until I get there. Do you know where he's staying?"

"He's at the Mission Inn down on Rio Road. You mean I can't make a citizen's arrest? Or have one of my busboys punch his lights out?"

"Wait until Reiko and I get back to Monterey. We'll be out of here in an hour. But I can't guarantee when we'll get back to the Peninsula."

Armand reluctantly agreed to follow my instructions, although I could sense his heartfelt need for revenge.

"Remember," I said, "this guy could be innocent. The evidence is circumstantial. Don't do anything rash."

"Pat, do me one favor. Do not tell the police there that I have their suspect in custody until it becomes vitally necessary."

"Are you asking me to obstruct justice, interfere with a police investigation?"

"That's what I'm asking."

"Okay. We never had this conversation. I'll see you—well, as soon as possible."

Reiko and I packed in a hurry. That is, I packed in a hurry and she had to conduct a search for all the little bits of stuff she had strewn around her room. Each of us had a fairly heavy rigid suitcase, but hers weighed twice as much as mine. I didn't have the courage to ask why.

I called Lieutenant Alvarez. "Is it okay to leave now? I mean, you don't need us for anything, do you?"

"No, Mr. Riordan. I believe we have everything under control now. I have just finished putting out a full alert for Applegate. We'll have our man in a short time. Have a pleasant trip."

Reiko insisted on driving us back to the airport. "You're pretty brave sometimes, Riordan, but you drive like a wimp."

About five minutes after we hit the freeway, I noticed a dark-colored sedan following us rather closely. Didn't think much of it at first, but then the guy in back gunned his motor until he touched our back bumper. I turned and craned my neck to see what was happening. I couldn't see the driver very well because of the tinted windshield, but he came up close again and this time bumped us a little harder.

"Uh-oh," said Reiko. "I've heard about this. These people look for rental cars and try to make 'em stop so they can mug people. That ain't gonna happen again, by God. I'll show 'em a couple of tricks."

By this time, the guy behind us had started to pull up alongside, and I could see he wasn't alone. A female with hard eyes was staring at us through the window on the passenger side. Reiko glanced to her left, put the pedal to the floor and took off.

Remember, this was an unfamiliar freeway in a city far, far from home. We were more or less under attack. My small partner was completely cool. We left the predator car in the dust, swung into the outside lane and passed four cars before zipping diagonally across traffic to take the offramp to the airport.

"How did you do that?" I asked.

"Easy pal. I read about these guys in the *Miami Herald*. So I knew what to do. I had studied the map before we left, so I knew where the offramp was. The whole thing was a breeze."

My heart was pounding when we pulled into the car rental lot, but Reiko was as serene as a morning in May. What would have happened if I had been driving? I don't know, honestly. I didn't know about these freeway pirates. One of 'em might have had a gun. One or both of us might have been killed. Another headline. Just another murder in Miami.

I will spare you the details of our trip from Miami to San Jose. We had to change at O'Hare in Chicago, one of the most noxious and frustrating airports in the nation, and our connecting flight was two hours late getting off the ground. There were thunderstorms during the entire trip, and the plane trembled constantly from "minor turbulence." But we made it.

It was after one o'clock in the morning when we reached the Monterey Peninsula. I drove over to Pacific Grove to drop Reiko off at her apartment, and went back to the cottage I occupy in Carmel. I don't think I slept fifteen minutes that night. Jet lag had been traumatic on the west-to-east flight. It shouldn't have been on the return. But as I lay on my bed trying to go to sleep, I kept going back over the days in Florida, somehow not at all satisfied with the clear-cut ending that this particular adventure seemed to have.

I climbed out of bed bleary-eyed when the sun came up and made a pot of coffee. There was an aged bagel in a paper bag on the sink, so I toasted it and smeared it with blueberry jam for breakfast.

The strength was coming back and the mind was beginning to clear. I called Tony Balestreri at the Monterey County Sheriff's Office.

"Riordan, it is 6 A.M. I have been on night duty all this week and I'm just about to go home and hit the sack. Why do you bug me this way?"

I told him the whole story of the Affair of the Restaurateur's Aunt, leaving out not one tiny detail.

"So, it's a done deal," he said. "What do you need me for?"

"It's just that I don't think this Applegate guy is necessarily the killer. Besides, who ever heard of a gigolo with a name like Applegate."

"Now that's a piece of fine logic, Pat. Go away and leave

me be. I refuse to get involved in another one of your convoluted murder cases."

"All I ask is that you keep an eye on the guy. He's in your jurisdiction, down at the Mission Inn."

"You mean the murder suspect is in Monterey County? What kind of a deal are you trying to pull, Riordan. I haven't checked recently, but there'll sure be a want on him from Miami. Do you expect me to keep my mouth shut about his whereabouts? You're nuts, pal."

"Don't check the wire, Tony. Just for a couple of days. I have a funny feeling about this whole mess, and I just want a couple of days. Okay?"

He grumbled, but said he'd go along. But just for a few days. "You're sure full of bullshit, Riordan," he said.

"That's right, buddy. Now go home and get some sleep."

I got dressed and took a walk down to Bruno's Market to get a couple of newspapers. It's my daily exercise when I'm home. Not going down to Bruno's. Coming up from Bruno's. The hill, as I've said before, provides enough of a cardiovascular workout for anyone. Sally often tells me she thinks it's the only reason my blood is still circulating.

At a reasonable hour I called Sally.

"What the hell do you mean you waited until a 'reasonable hour'?" She was overjoyed to hear from me. "I'm not out of bed yet, you cretin. You think I'm glad to hear that you're home safe? Well, I guess I am."

"Let's have lunch, Sal. I'm bursting to relate to you the details of my trip. Especially since you arranged all the details." I may have sounded a bit sarcastic.

"You're kidding, aren't you? You had a rotten trip and you're going to blame me for everything, aren't you? Pick me up at my office at eleven-thirty." She hung up.

Should I tell her that Reiko had seduced me at that miserable airport hotel? Maybe that the two of us had nonstop passion at Howard Johnson's, tearing each other's clothes off and showering together?

She wouldn't believe it. That's a damn shame, I thought. She knows me too well.

Much later, I called Armand.

"Do you know of any enemies your aunt might have had?"

He thought a moment. "Not really. But I haven't seen her for several years. She hasn't mentioned any trouble in any of our telephone conversations. But she was very well fixed, Pat. Nobody in the family knows just how much money she had, but she was generally presumed to be loaded. She wouldn't get out of that little house in Miami Shores. She had lived in it off and on for forty-five years. And, although we were aware that the neighborhood had changed a good deal, none of us was able to persuade her to move."

"How about a will? Is there such a thing?"

"Oh, yes. I got a call yesterday from her attorney. He's sending us all the details by Federal Express. I'll know more some time today."

"Let me know when it comes, Armand. It could be helpful."

"I'll call you. Bye-bye. Hey, wait a minute, Pat. I got another call yesterday. From one of Therese's acquaintances back there. She and another friend of my aunt's are coming out here. She sounded a little spooky. And she told me there were things I ought to know about Therese. The two are flying to San Francisco and they expect me to meet them. I can't, of course, but I'll send somebody. You want to know when they arrive?"

"You bet. I'll be at the office in an hour. You can get me there until five or six."

At first I found that pretty amusing. I mean, that a couple of Aunt Therese's friends were on their way to California. But I found out very soon that there wasn't much that was funny about their mission.

# 9

# "Is this Flora Grimme?"

WHEN I ROLLED into the office that morning I was startled not to find Reiko sitting at her computer, summoning up some sort of exotic information. She does things like that for her own amusement, I think.

She has a link to one of those world-wide services upon which one may call for anything from quotations from the New York Stock Exchange to the real low-down on the sex life of anchovies. When she isn't doing something for what we laughingly call the company, she's educating herself on, say, the history of vampires.

I was disappointed not to find her. There was no sign that she had been in and ducked out for coffee. The office was sterile and bleak without her and a sudden wave of melancholy swept over me.

Then I looked at the phone machine.

The thing was blinking furiously, as if it were about to burst. I hit the button, grabbed a pad and pencil and sat down heavily on Reiko's knee-stool, a move that never fails to make me aware of my coccyx.

"Mr. Riordan, this is Flora Grimme. My jewelry has been stolen. All of it. Please call." The woman left a number which I jotted on the pad. Before I finished writing the number, the same voice came again: "Mr. Riordan, Flora Grimme calling. Please call." Same number.

Every damn call—there were six or seven—was the same. This Grimme woman sounded a little more hysterical with every message. The last one was so shrill as to be almost unintelligible.

I called the lady. She answered before the end of the first ring.

"Hello, hello. Who's there, please?"

"Is this Flora Grimme?" I asked. "Pat Riordan. You called?" There was a moan from the other end of the line.

"Oh, thank God. Mr. Riordan, I am a friend of George Spelvin here in Pebble Beach. George said that he had no doubt that you could help me."

"That's kind of George, Flora, but I don't know what kind of help you need. You said something about jewelry?"

"Yes, Mr. Riordan. I recently returned from the south of France, where I had been visiting for the first few months of the year. When I got home, I discovered that the strongbox containing all of my jewelry was missing. All of it. Including the perfect thirty carat diamond that the late Mr. Grimme had given me."

"Just a minute, Flora. This is a burglary case. Have you called the Sheriff's Office? I'm a private investigator, you know. Burglary is something quite out of my area of expertise. Give me a missing person, an insurance scam, a piece of industrial espionage, I'm your man. But for burglary, you've got the wrong number."

"Please help me. The Sheriff's men have been here. They've found nothing. There was no sign of a break-in. There were no fingerprints. They just scratch their heads and say that they'll do their best, but they've got little to go on. They're very nice men, Mr. Riordan, but my jewelry is still missing."

"Wasn't it insured? Have you called your insurance company?"

There was a moment of silence. "It was not insured. I was not about to have some insurance agent nosing about in my house, examining my jewel collection."

"That's not the way it's done, Flora. All you do is get an appraisal from an authorized jewelry appraiser and you pay so much per thousand valuation. Haven't you ever had the stuff appraised?"

"Yes, of course. But I do not trust insurance people. I have not trusted them since my last accident. They canceled my automobile insurance. Because of those accidents. And none of them were my fault, mind you."

Uh-oh. The realization that I was dealing with a nut began to creep into my brain.

"What kind of accidents, Flora? What did they cancel you for?"

"They didn't exactly cancel me. Just cut me to the bare minimum for liability. But it was completely unfair."

This conversation was getting nowhere, so I made another attempt to get off the hook.

"I'm sorry, Flora. I really cannot help you. You're just going to have to sweat out the Sheriff."

"Please, Mr.Riordan," she was pleading now, "if nothing else, just come out here to talk to me. George said you're a very nice man. He said you had helped him a great deal."

I sighed. "Okay, Flora. When's a good time? I'll come, but I won't promise anything."

"Thank you. I will pay any amount you ask. Come any morning. But call first, please. My personal trainer is here Mondays, Wednesdays and Fridays."

She's gonna pay me, I thought. I can use the money. I agreed to look in on Flora Grimme one day the following week.

At that moment, Reiko walked in.

"God, I was bushed. I haven't slept so well in years. Hit that old sack and went out of it like right away. How're you?"

I waxed indignant. "I did not sleep worth a good goddam. Look at my eyes, kid. Red. Baggy. Unclosed for hours. Called Tony at six this morning and got snapped at for my pains. And now some ditsy woman from Pebble Beach wants me to investigate a jewel theft."

"Didja tell her to call the cops?"

"Do I look like an idiot? Of course, I told her to call the cops. She had already called the cops. They told her they couldn't do anything. And it wasn't the cops, it was the Sheriff."

"What are you going to do?"

"The woman offered to pay me. I will drive out to PB and talk to her when I get a chance. I will take her money and hold her hand and tell her to kiss her diamonds goodbye. That's what I'll do."

"You're some kind of case, Riordan," said Reiko. "You don't anticipate doing anything for the lady, and you'll take her money."

"She insisted, goddammit. George told her to call me. I owe George. What else?"

She clucked and shook her head. "Get off my chair, pal. I've got things to do."

I rose and with as much dignity as I could muster, went into my office. Two minutes later the phone rang.

"It's Armand," Reiko called to me. "Pick it up."

# 10
## *I had not expected to witness such a scene.*

MY FIRST MEETING with Herman Applegate shocked the hell out of me. Somehow, I had anticipated an oily type with slick black hair and a toothbrush mustache, a smiling gigolo with glittering, rapacious eyes. The real Herman turned out to be a middle-aged, balding guy in a bad suit, pathetically eager to please even me.

"Pleased to meet you, Mr. Riordan," he said, after Armand had introduced us. We were in the restaurant office. Armand had not wasted any time in his call to me. "Come here now," he had demanded. He's hard to resist when he demands.

Looking a little puzzled but completely unlike a criminal who had fled the scene of an especially gruesome crime, Applegate sat looking at Armand and me with faded and rheumy blue eyes.

"Armand told me we have some important business to discuss. Are you his attorney, Mr. Riordan?"

"No. Well, yes, I *am* an attorney. That is, I have a law

Roy Gilligan

degree. But I don't practice law. I . . . I sort of assist in legal matters, you might say." I was stumbling. I still didn't know why Armand had summoned me so abruptly or how much he had told Applegate.

Armand was grim. He had said nothing since his perfunctory ritual of introduction. He fixed Applegate with a cold stare. When he spoke, his words were precise. Although he has lived in the U.S. most of his life, when he is deadly serious, his speech takes on an unidentifiable European accent, common to people who have routinely spoken several languages throughout their lives.

"Mr. Applegate, when you arrived here last week, you told me that you and my Aunt Therese were engaged to be married, and that she was to follow you in a short while."

"Why, yes, Armand. Therese told me that she had already made the plane reservations, that we might *stay* in California if she liked it here. We ought to see her any day now."

Armand's face flushed. "Applegate, you are a liar. And you are much worse. You're a murderer. You are perfectly aware that my aunt is dead, because you killed her. *Killed* her, left her dead on the floor of her house. And came here to extort money from me." He was on his feet and his voice had risen to a shout that could easily be heard above the traffic noise on Fifth Avenue outside the office's only window.

I had not expected to witness such a scene. "Armand, buddy, I asked you not to do this. I know you're pretty upset about your aunt's death, but this just ain't the way." I looked at Applegate.

All the life had gone out of the man's face. His mouth gaped open and he looked at Armand in total disbelief. His hands began to tremble, ever so slightly at first. The shaking quickly got worse and spread to his entire body. He grasped the arms of his chair as if to keep from collapsing. The chair legs rattled against the plain vinyl on Armand's office floor.

Armand's face lost some of its hostility as he watched Applegate simply fall apart before his eyes. I moved to the man's aid and threw my arms around his shoulders to keep him from falling forward. The whole nerve-wracking episode seemed to go on for several minutes.

At last, there was a stillness in the office. Armand sat down and stared across his desk at the man who had earlier been so pleasant and cheerful. I was still hanging onto Applegate, but the terrible shaking had stopped.

Armand spoke to me: "You have seen his reaction, Pat. It is an admission of guilt, of course. I asked you to come here as a witness. This trembling wretch killed my aunt. You can see that, can't you?"

"I can't see anything except that this poor bastard has just about fallen apart. I was afraid you'd do something like this, Armand. Frankly, this man does not strike me as a criminal who has just been confronted with his crime. He looks to me like a guy who has just been told the worst news he has heard in his life."

Applegate's gaze was fixed on a marble paperweight that Armand kept on his desk. He was completely silent and motionless. I couldn't hear him breathe. I moved around in front of him, still hanging onto one shoulder, and bent down to look him full in the face. "Herman, say something. Were you telling the truth about you and Therese? Were you really engaged? The lady must have been twenty or twenty-five years older than you. What's the story?"

Herman Applegate came out of his momentary trance. His voice was flat and dull, unlike the cheery tones in which he had acknowledged meeting me. "Therese is dead. She was so kind to me. She *said* she didn't love me. And she didn't. But I loved her. In a way. But I didn't kill her. I *couldn't* have killed her. She was about to rescue me from . . . myself."

If I had let go of the guy, I'm sure he would have fallen forward. He was no lightweight, and my arm was getting pretty tired holding him up. He found the strength to raise his head and look me in the eyes. "Look at me. I don't have to tell you that I was not the most popular escort in the agency. I sure as hell don't look like much. I've got good manners and I'm nice to old ladies. Therese told me that was all she needed. She was going to leave me a lot of money. All I had to do was marry her and look after her. Marriage was something she'd never tried, she said. But at her age, she needed someone to take care of her. Jesus, I couldn't kill her. And I can't imagine who could."

I turned on Armand. "Have you called the police? Have you said anything to anybody but me about this mess?"

He shook his head. "This man is guilty. Anyone can see that."

"I don't think so, Armand. This man is no prizewinnner. In some respects, he's not much of a man. But believe me, he doesn't act like a killer, either."

# 11
## *Armand's face was almost purple.*

WHEN I MET Maybelle Carothers and Veronica Small, I was transported in a flash to the early '70s and a short-run TV show called "The Snoop Sisters," which starred two wonderful actresses, Helen Hayes and Mildred Natwick. I could never figure out why that show wasn't more of a success. But then, I'm pretty much at a loss as to how most television shows got on the air in the first place. Oh, I watch the box quite a lot. I'm a single guy, living alone. At my age, what else? Sally Morse won't marry me.

But Maybelle and Veronica were standing in Armand's office, mainly because there weren't enough chairs to accomodate everybody, when I walked in, summoned by my client in haste, just like the last time. Armand was standing, too, out of common politeness, I guess. Sizing up the situation with my cool, analytical mind, I just stayed in the doorway.

Armand performed the introductions. "These ladies have flown out here at their own expense, Pat. They feel that since

Therese was their special friend, they ought to do something. They tell me that they have information that can help us. I asked them to save it until I could call you. You understand."

"Nice meeting you, ladies," I said, with what I believed to be a charming smile. "But, Armand, isn't there somewhere where we can all sit down?"

He looked blank for a moment. Then, as if divine inspiration had struck him, he said: "Yes, of course. It is three o'clock in the afternoon. There should be very few people in the restaurant. Let's go down into the patio." He struggled from behind his desk and led us out the door.

The pleasant, sunlit patio was nearly deserted. A young couple, probably newlyweds, was lingering over a bottle of expensive wine in a corner, but the rest of the tables were empty. The young man and woman were locked together at the knees, sipping the wine from narrow, stemmed glasses and holding hands. They were blissfully unaware of the four of us at a table across the patio.

"Would anyone like something to drink. A glass of wine? Coffee? Iced tea?" Armand was determined to seem the perfect gentleman.

Maybelle spoke for the first time since mumbling an acknowledgement to our introduction. "It's damn cold out here. Do we have to stay here? If we do, I want some coffee. With a little brandy. Veronica'll have the same."

"I am sorry, Mrs. Carothers, my restaurant does not serve distilled beverages. We have only wine." Armand was being gracious, but I could sense an undercurrent of annoyance. "And we will be able to talk more freely out here. My restaurant help is setting up for dinner inside. And the place is rather small."

"Very well, then. Coffee. Black, as strong as you got it. Veronica'll have the same."

Armand signalled a waiter and ordered coffee for all of us. When it had been served, he turned to me. "Pat, I think it will be better if you conduct this interview. The ladies are here.

They believe they have information that will shed light on my aunt's murder. I am convinced that the Applegate fellow is guilty. But I will listen."

I searched my mind for a way to begin. But it turned out that I didn't have to. Maybelle Carothers took over.

"Therese was a dear friend. She was tight as hell with her money and she could be real standoffish, but she was a dear friend. She was Veronica's dear friend, too, wasn't she, Veronica. Yes, indeed."

Veronica, who had not said a word since we sat down around the table, nodded and smiled a tiny, wistful smile.

Maybelle went on: "Anyhow, we didn't like that gigolo of hers, that Herman Applegate. Oh, he didn't seem like a dangerous person. But he was hangin' around too much, you know what I mean? He was a . . . a . . . a opportunist, I think you'd say. But I don't think he killed her. No, he didn't have guts enough to kill her. He was a bad man. He coulda blackmailed her or conned her, but he wouldn't have killed her. I'm sure of that."

While she was talking, I had a chance to get a good look at the two ladies from Florida. Both had carefully coiffed white hair. Both wore flowered print dresses. Both had short jackets which they pulled tightly around them in the Carmel chill. Each lady carried an enormous purse, bulging with God knows what. And yet, they seemed very different. Maybelle was perhaps two or three inches the taller, and considerably heavier. She had prominent features, accented with heavy black eyebrows. Veronica, on the other hand, had a soft, unlined face and looked out at the world with wide brown eyes. I wondered if she ever got to speak for herself in the presence of the formidable Mrs. Carothers. She nodded and smiled as Maybelle went on.

"Therese called me about a week before she died. She didn't call me very often. Usually, I had to call her. But when she did call, she most often wanted something. But the last time—the week before she died, remember—she said she was real happy. She and this Applegate were going to California and get married. He'd gone on ahead, she said. And *then* she told me something else. She had called one of her relatives in California to tell 'em about it—she didn't say if it was a him or a her—and the relative sort of hit the ceiling on the telephone, if you can do that. Seems the relative told her to stay put, and he—or she—would fly back and try to talk her out of marrying this Applegate. But she wasn't going to back down. That Therese. She knew what she wanted. And she'd had what she wanted all her life. Veronica and me, we're her age, y'know. We never had anything like what Therese had. But we're not here to complain. It just seems like to us that that Applegate, lyin' sonofabitch that he is, did not kill Therese. But we think we know who did, don't we Veronica? It was that relative from California."

Armand's face twisted in disbelief. At the beginning of the woman's monologue he had leaned forward, expectantly. As her story unfolded, his expression grew more and more incredulous. I'm just guessing, but I think what was going through his head was something like, "This old bitch is out of her bloody mind."

I had to say something. "Thank you, Mrs. Carothers. You say you don't have any idea whether Therese's visitor from California was a man or a woman? No clue? Therese didn't say anything that would give you a hint?"

"Nothing. Just a relative. Somebody in her will, or somebody who wanted to be in her will. Some thieving relative."

Armand's face was almost purple. His hands were clenched into fists. When he spoke, his voice was low and tense:

"You ladies came all the way out here to tell me that my aunt was killed by a relative. Don't you realize that a relative of hers *has* to be a relative of mine? Are you accusing *me*?"

"You been to Miami recently?" asked Maybelle.

Armand exploded. "No! I haven't been out of Carmel for *months!* Please leave my restaurant! I will not be accused in my own restaurant."

I had to do something. "Hold it, Armand. I don't think that these ladies would have come here to accuse you to your face. But they do know something, obviously." I turned to Veronica, who sat silent, still smiling her tiny smile. "How about you, Mrs. Small? Can you add anything to what Mrs. Carothers has told us?"

Veronica looked at Armand and then at me. She glanced quickly at Maybelle. She fingered the leather strap on her handbag and touched her moussed and molded hairdo. Finally, she spoke:

"I never heard from Therese. But I live just up the street from her house. And about a week before her body was found, I saw somebody go up to her door and ring the bell. She let the person in. Mind you, I wasn't too close. But it looked like a tall, dark-haired man in a gray suit. I never saw him come out."

Veronica looked at all of us, one at a time, and smiled. Armand sat back in his chair with his eyes rolled up and his mouth open. I tried to think of a way out of this mess. Maybelle just glared.

# 12
## *"Riordan, you're sort of a pig, y'know."*

"SO WHERE was this Applegate guy all this time? In jail? On his way back to Miami? You're leaving a lot of holes, Riordan." Reiko had been listening to my tale of the ladies from Florida. She was the very picture of skepticism. As usual, she thought I was a little nuts and had conducted myself badly in the interview.

"Applegate is at the Mission Inn, probably crying his eyes out. He has sworn to stay put, as long as Armand pays the hotel bill. Armand, on the other hand, has many friends, some of whom are in management at the Mission Inn. They've sworn to keep a close eye on Herman. So that's taken care of."

She frowned. "Does the Sheriff know about this? Have you called Tony Balestreri?" Balestreri isn't the only sergeant in the Sheriff's Office in Monterey County, but he's the only one I can lie to. He *knows* I lie to him, but he accepts it.

"Yes, honey, but I didn't tell him everything. There's no

reason to bring the authorities into this yet. Those two ladies who represent themselves as close friends of the murdered woman have implicated one of Armand's relatives as the killer. This could be damned embarrassing, if not tragic. No. No cops yet. We've got to explore all possibilities. I know most of Armand's family. I can't think of any one of 'em who might be homicidal."

"Well, did you *ask* him if there might be a black sheep? Hell, maybe there's a third or fourth cousin floating around out there who might have had a long-standing grudge agains Therese."

She sure is persistent. Gets her teeth into something and just won't let go. Really bugs the hell out of me sometimes. But she makes me a better investigator. Maybe I resent *that*.

"Reiko-san, I didn't think it wise to push Armand too hard at the moment. He calmed down pretty quick. But he wasn't what you'd call polite to the two ladies. He dumped them off on me and said to take 'em anywhere they wanted to go. Before I could tell him that I was no goddam taxi driver, he shoved us all out of the patio."

"And what did you do with them? Put 'em on the next plane back to Miami?"

"I drove them to the Doubletree. Armand's man had picked them up at the airport, and they hadn't checked in anywhere yet. They got real chummy on the way. Wanted to see Cannery Row and Fisherman's Wharf. Damn, I felt like a tour guide. Made me wonder if the girls were making the whole thing up to justify the trip. The big one—Maybelle—gave me an affectionate hug at the hotel. It was stifling, sort of like having a perfumed pillow pushed in your face. The little one just giggled."

"So, what do we do now, exalted investigator? Sit back and relax? Let the chips fall where they may? My granddad had a saying something like that, only it was in Japanese."

"Reiko, are you willing to opt out of this case after having found the old lady's corpse in that crummy house? Hell no, you're not. What I want you to do—as carefully as possible—is to snoop around and find out if there are any collateral Colbert relatives on the Peninsula. That ought to be fairly easy."

"I don't need you to make anything easy for me, O mighty one." She clapped on the shapeless cotton hat she wears in windy weather and stomped out of the office. Before she reached the outside door, she turned and said: "Riordan, you're sort of a pig, y'know. I wouldn't be workin' at your side if I didn't love you a little. 'Bye. I'll be back late in the afternoon."

I sat back in my chair and thought about what she said. Reiko had never said she *loved* me before, even a little. Well, that kind of spelled out our relationship. It isn't passionately physical, and it isn't a father-daughter thing. It's just that we love each other—a little.

The telephone made one of its obnoxious electronic noises. God, where have all the old bells gone?

I picked it up. "Riordan and Masuda, can I help you?"

"This is Maybelle Carothers, Mr. Riordan. I have just remembered something. I guess me and Veronica were both a little fuzzy from the plane trip. Therese didn't tell me it was a real relative she called. It was somebody who was just *like* a relative. Somebody she told me was as close to her as any of her real relatives, but somebody she didn't like very much. Matter of fact, somebody she got a real kick out of disinheriting. Does that help you any? I'm sorry we made Mr. Colbert mad, but, sweetie, when you get to a certain age, sometimes you forget things, or remember them wrong."

"Thank you, Maybelle. Yes, it does help a lot. Now we know that it could be almost anybody in California. That means we've only got about thirty million suspects. Shouldn't take long to sift 'em down. Have a good day."

It also meant that I had sent my partner off in pursuit of a wild goose.

# 13
## *"Somebody stole my car, my Civic."*

I CALLED Armand.

"Hey, pal, is there anybody that you can come up with who would have been 'just like a relative' to Therese? Maybe in New York. Maybe in Florida. Maybe here. Search your brain."

"What? Riordan, are you absolutely insane? Can you seriously ask such a question? Therese was my favorite aunt. You know that. But I saw her only on widely separated occasions during my lifetime. She was in show business. She traveled a lot. She had lots of friends. Make that lots of acquaintances. I'm not sure about the friends. How in God's name am I expected to remember somebody who was 'just like a relative' to Therese?"

"I dunno, Armand." I heaved a mighty sigh. "Maybe we should start with the *real* relatives and use the process of elimination. Like Sherlock Holmes said. Eliminate all the real relatives and, whether you like it or not, what's left will be the likely suspects. Or words to that effect."

There was a considerable silence. I could hear Armand's teeth grinding.

"You know, don't you, that I have lost both my parents. My brothers all live on the Monterey Peninsula, as do my sisters. None of them has left the area in the last six months. I can prove that. There is one uncle, who still lives in Belgium, but he is hopelessly crippled and has never been in the United States. There is an aunt who is eighty-six and lives in San Francisco. She has a very small apartment out in the Avenues, and seldom leaves it. That's it. Nobody else. Nobody. The whole family."

I thanked him and the conversation was ended. It had borne no fruit whatsoever.

Veronica Small had told us that she had seen a tall, dark-haired man knock on Therese's door and be admitted. She had not seen him come out. And the time-frame was right. It was about a week before Reiko and I arrived to discover the body. Applegate? Hell no, Herman was overweight and dumpy and didn't have much hair. Armand had accounted for all of his relatives. Who could the guy have been?

I heard the office door slam, and Reiko stormed into my sanctum sanctorum with fury in her face.

"Somebody stole my car, my Civic. Some filthy sonofabitch hot-wired my car and drove it away. Why would anybody do that, Riordan? Why would anybody steal a Honda Civic? And right off Washington Street, across from the Bank of America. I just moved it an hour ago. Aw, shit!"

"Have you perchance missed a payment, Reiko-san? Finance people are really picky about that, y'know. They send out guys whose only *raison d'être* is to repossess cars for delinquent payments."

"I paid cash for the car! You know that. I traded in the old Mustang and paid cash. What'll I do now?" She sat down, rather heavily for such a petite woman, and put her face in her hands.

"Call the cops. Call the Sheriff's Office. Right now, before the guy gets all the way to Oregon. You *do* have insurance, don't you?"

She raised her tear-stained face to me. "Yes. I have insurance. I'm covered." The fury was gone, and pure misery had taken its place.

I felt a deep pain as I looked at that sad little face. It's so easy to tell somebody what to do when that person's travail is none of yours. I stood up and walked around the desk and stood behind her, stroking her glossy black hair with my hands. "Hey, honey," I said, "it's just a car. The cops will find it. Probably. But if they don't, the insurance company will buy you another one. Don't cry."

"It's not the car so much, Riordan. It's the personalized plates. I had to fight to get 'em. And now they're *gone*. I'll never get license plates like that again."

I went back around the desk and sat down. I could understand a trauma about losing a friend or a relative—or even a car—but having an emotional outburst over the loss of a couple of California personalized license plates was more than I could take.

"Go call the authorities, babe. Tell 'em you don't need the car, but you'd like to have the plates. Tell 'em to be sure and cover both sides of the 101 Freeway in case the perpetrator cast off the license plates to avoid detection."

She went meekly back to her desk and picked up the phone.

I called out to her: "And don't bother to look for any Colbert relatives. They're all accounted for."

The easiest thing to do at this point, I reflected, would be just to dismiss the information from the two old ladies from Florida, and forget about the whole affair, which I was on the verge of doing.

But one thing was gnawing at me. If I didn't make an effort to find the killer of Therese Colbert, poor old Herman Applegate would get hanged for the murder, or whatever they do in Florida, and a real killer would go free. The evidence against Herman was purely circumstantial. But his finger-prints on the knife that looked like the murder weapon was evidence enough for some juries. And if Herman couldn't prove he was maybe in a hot tub with an amorous client at the time of the murder, he would be, as we used to say in the army, "shit outa luck."

Yeah, I could have just said t'hell with it. I didn't owe anything to Herman. I didn't even like him much. But there was just something so pitiful about him that I couldn't let him take a bad rap.

So I was stuck. But I didn't have a suspect. And I didn't have a clue. Until I got that long distance call from Alvarez in Miami.

# 14
## *"Sir, you are obstructing justice."*

"MR. RIORDAN? It is Lieutenant Alvarez from Miami. You do remember me?"

"Sure, Lieutenant. We had some pretty interesting conversations about a dead body I found. How the hell could I *not* remember you?"

A sound like a strangulated chuckle came across the continent. "Yes, I think you recognize my name. It might interest you to know that we have discovered that Miss Colbert had a visitor a week before you arrived and that the visitor was not Mr. Applegate, who, of course, is still our prime suspect."

"I know that." This guy was beginning to get on my nerves a bit. He had this way of dramatizing—even over the phone— any bit of information. Sort of like a character in a TV soap opera who appears only on Fridays and sets the hook for the following week. But this time I had surprised him.

"How could you know?" He was honestly shaken up. "We only turned up this information yesterday, knocking on doors in the lady's neighborhood. You have been gone from here for more than a week."

I told the Lieutenant about the two ditsy ladies who had flown out to tell Armand what they knew.

"We've got the girls stashed in a hotel in Monterey. And, by the way, Applegate's here, too. That poor bastard doesn't seem to know his ass from third base, anyhow. No, Alvarez, Herman just ain't the killer. He'd have a tough time setting out roach traps, let alone murdering an old woman with a kitchen knife. But what about this visitor? Anybody identify him?"

"I'm afraid not, Mr. Riordan, although a lady who lives across the street said she had seen him before, several times. Wait a minute! Did you say that Applegate is *there*? You have known about this for some time? Sir, you are obstructing justice. He is still our *number one suspect*. You were obligated to tell the authorities of his presence." The reaction was delayed, but vehement. Alvarez was shouting at me now.

"Hold off, Lieutenant. The authorities here have been notified." I lied a little there. "Besides, if you could see this whimpering clod, you'd know he couldn't have done the deed. So, what do we do about the new guy?"

He calmed down. "We have a description. A tall man with dark hair, wearing a gray suit. A business type. A real estate agent perhaps. Or an insurance salesman. That's for descriptive purposes, of course. We are fairly sure that the deceased was not interested in selling the house she had lived in for forty-five years, and I don't think at her age she was insurable."

"Okay, what are you doing to try to find this unknown gray suit?"

"We are continuing to question neighbors and people who frequent the neighborhood. Delivery people, trash collectors and the like. So far, nothing. By the way, what's to become of the house? I have a cousin who might be interested in buying it."

"You'll have to get in touch with Armand Colbert, the lady's nephew." I gave him Armand's address.

"Thank you, Mr. Riordan. Uh, I assume your local authorities will be in touch with us. About Applegate, I mean. He must be returned to Dade County, you know."

"You may rest assured they'll be in touch, Lieutenant." I wasn't a damn bit sure about that, but it was just a small lie.

Alvarez and I said a fond *adios,* and hung up.

So now we have a guy in a gray suit, tall, with dark hair. Veronica had told us about him, and now some other neighbor had told Alvarez or one of his minions.

So there was another person involved. Another person at Therese's door. Could have been just somebody selling something. But how the hell were we going to find out?

Alvarez had ruled out a real estate agent. Maybe not. Maybe Therese, anticipating her marriage and taking up residence in California, did intend to sell the house on 92nd street. Hey, wasn't that an old movie? "The House on 92nd Street?" Or she was doing some business with an insurance agent. Or something else.

I don't know why it took me so long to think of the other possibilities. It should have been perfectly obvious. Therese was straightening up her affairs. She was arranging her estate. The visitor could well have been her stockbroker. Or her attorney. Her will? Had she made her will? Was she making some changes to take care of Herman?

Armand was expecting to hear from Therese's attorney about her estate. I knocked the telephone to the floor in my haste to call him.

"I'm sorry, Mr. Riordan. Mr. Colbert's aunt's lawyer just arrived in town and they left about a half hour ago. Is there a message?" Armand's manager was a sweet voiced young lady of considerable appeal.

"Do you know where they went?"

"I'm not really sure. When Mr. Colbert leaves here he sometimes has lunch at The Lodge. You might try to find him there."

The Lodge in Pebble Beach. Ah, yes, Armand would take a visiting attorney to lunch at The Lodge.

I put on a necktie that I keep in the bottom drawer of my desk for special occasions. It bore tiny stains from some of the best restaurants in town. The day was warm, but I took a seldom-worn blazer from a hook on the wall and, barking my shins on the elephant's foot umbrella stand, dashed out of the office.

# 15
## *"My jewelry has been stolen."*

BEFORE I COULD reach the staircase, however, I was confronted by the largest woman I had ever seen. She wasn't obese, you understand, or tall and skinny. She was just *big*. I had always thought that Sally Morse was a good-sized girl because she could look me straight in the eye, even with low heels. But this lady towered. She was ample of bosom and wide of hip, but nevertheless in perfect balance. She emerged from the staircase and stood stock-still in front of me. I skidded to a halt.

"Can you direct me to the office of Patrick Riordan, the private investigator?" she asked.

The temptation was strong to say that the poor guy had been evicted for non-payment of rent, but I had a notion that I would have to admit the untruth somewhere down the line.

"I'm Pat Riordan. Uh, how can I help you, madam?"

She pinned both of my arms against my body with hands like Arnold Schwarzenegger's. "Thank God. I am Flora

Grimme. You promised to help me. I could wait no longer. Can we talk?"

"Sure," I said, weakly. "This is my office. Right here. You can let go now."

I led Flora into Reiko's half of the office, turned and faced Flora Grimme. She crowded me until I was sitting on the edge of Reiko's desk.

"As I told you on the phone, Flora, there isn't a heck of a lot I can do, but I can run out to your place next week and look around."

She had a large face and a large head to go with that large body. Her features were oversized as well. The eyes were very dark and the white showed all around the iris, giving her a spooky, staring look. Her nose was, to put it kindly, prominent, and her mouth was wide and brilliant red. She wore the kind of hat that I think they call a *cloche,* something that I thought had gone out of style a few decades ago. What I could see of her hair was dead white. It wasn't silvery or blonde, just dead white. She was the kind of person, male or female, that I wouldn't want to meet in the dark of night on a deserted street. Something about her just plain scared the hell out of me.

"My jewelry has been stolen. It was worth upwards of two million dollars. I want it back. I want you to get it back for me."

Her stare never wavered.

Maybe if I showed a little interest: "Flora, was there anything else missing when your stuff was taken? Like money, silverware, valuable paintings."

"Nothing. Just my fabulous jewelry. All gone, all gone." She sounded mournful, but her face might just as well have been carved in stone.

"May I ask, Flora, if there is a Mr. Grimme? Are you married?"

"Not at the moment. I have had three husbands, the last of which I kicked out of my house six months ago. He was a leech, that one. The first two were money-grubbing bastards, but that last one was just a leech."

"Does any of those guys have a key to the house? Did they know where you kept your jewels?"

"I had all locks changed after I got rid of each of them. I have changed the location of my strongbox weekly. Now in the back of my closet, then in the wine cellar. Even submerged in the hot tub. I made sure it was waterproof, of course."

This thing was beginning to take on a surreal feeling. The big woman hadn't moved since she backed me into the desk. I was anxious to get out to The Lodge to catch Armand and Therese's lawyer. In a sort of panic, I made an unwise commitment: "Flora, I've really got to see the scene of the crime. I promise that I will call you and come out to your house next week. Just now I have a pressing engagement. Will you excuse me, please?"

She slowly backed off. "How old are you, Riordan?" she asked.

That took me completely by surprise. "Really, Flora, I don't see what difference it makes. I'm . . . mature. I've been around a good while. I've been in this business over thirty years. Why do you ask?"

She squinted at me, stepped back two paces, and looked me up and down.

"The shoes are terrible. You have no crease in your pants. The jacket is, well, really abominable. And there are many stains on your tie. But you might do. Are you married, Mr. Riordan?"

My God, I thought. Is she sizing me up for husband number four? The feeling I had can only be described as abject terror.

She turned abruptly and walked toward the door. As she was about to leave, she turned and pinned me with those eyes. "You'll call me. Next week. Or *I'll* call *you*."

My life has not been what you might call a bed of roses. But Flora Grimme filled me with a gnawing fear that I hadn't experienced since I heard the Red Chinese were just over the hill in Korea.

But I had to pull myself together and get out to Pebble Beach.

# 16
## *But I was rich!*

THE GUY at the Pebble Beach gate at the top of Carmel
Hill tried to charge me the tourist rate, but I conned him out
of it.

"Dammit, I'm the guest of George Spelvin. You know
*George Spelvin!* Gray-haired guy with big bucks. Drives a
Bentley with a special body. He wouldn't want me to have to
pay."

"Go right ahead, sir. Sorry, sir." Polite guy, right? But I
heard him call after me as I drove off, "You might get that
thing washed, though, and have some of the dings removed."
My little Mercedes two-seater backfired derisively.

For your information, George is for real, except that it ain't
his right name. I never identify George to strangers. He has
blood of purest azure hue, but he also has a penchant for
marrying the wrong women.

I help him now and then, and he lets me stay in my little
Carmel cottage, rent free. But recently—and I haven't even

told Reiko this—I've been thinking of getting a place of my own.

It came as a complete shock to me that I had over $50,000 in the bank. I honestly don't even remember *putting* it in the bank. If you had asked me three months ago if I had any money, I'd have told you I was flat broke.

It was like this: The phone rang one day and it was this person from a branch of the Bank of America in San Francisco. The caller asked me some gentle, cautious questions. Was I the Patrick Riordan who maintained offices in the Flood Building? Yeah, but I moved five or six years ago. And it was only a one-room operation. "Ah," the voice continued, "you must be the person. We have a certificate of deposit in your name that's maturing. We have sent you notice, but we get back our mail to you with a yellow sticker that says 'forwarding address expired'. Where are you?"

Wouldn't that grab you? I mean, to suddenly know you've got a bank account with actual *money* in it. In your own name.

"How much money?" I asked, after holding my breath as long as I could.

"Fifty-two thousand, seven hundred and thirty-two dollars and sixty-one cents. The interest has accumulated for some time, you see. But we *do* have to know what you want us to do with the money."

"Put it in an envelope and mail it here. Better still, send it Federal Express." I was freaked out. The person asked for information for purposes of identification: my mother's maiden name, my social security number, all that jazz.

But I was rich! And slowly it came back to me. When my wife was killed in an auto accident long years back, she left an insurance policy of $100,000, doubled for accidental death. Living through the next couple of years in an alcoholic haze, I concluded when I finally got sober that I had spent all the money. Among other events that I could not remember that occurred during that time was a brief period of sobriety during which I had the good sense to put some of the money in the bank.

So, I'm thinking about getting a little place of my own. Got to tell Reiko. Got to tell Sally. Especially Sally. She mignt consider marrying me if I buy a house.

But I digress. People are always yelling at me for digressing.

When I got to The Lodge it was easy to find Armand and his guest. They were at a quiet corner table in the dining room, apparently involved in a hushed but intense conversation.

Armand looked up as I approached.

"How did you find me?" He seemed annoyed. "No matter. Patrick Riordan, this is Elliott Sterns, my recently deceased aunt's attorney. From Miami. This is the man I've been telling you about, Elliott. The private investigator I sent to Florida."

Sterns rose to his feet. Tall, dark hair, gray suit. About fifty, I'd judge. He extended his hand and made his face smile.

"Pleasure, Pat. Armand has a lot of confidence in you, apparently. I only wish you could have come into my office when you were in Miami."

"I sure wish I had met you back there, Elliott. We might have been able to clear up a few things. The only thing we really know is that you visited Therese several times shortly before her death."

He was just a wee bit startled by my speculative remark. I didn't *really* know he was the guy Therese's friends and neighbors were talking about, but, on the other hand, it was worth a shot.

"Ah, yes, I *did* pay a few calls on the poor lady just before she was killed. She was interested in liquidating some of her holdings and making a new will. I, on the other hand, was interested in talking her out of marrying this hired escort she had been seeing. Wonderful lady, you understand, but stubborn. When she had her mind made up about anything, it was impossible to change it."

"What changes did she make in the will? Did she take care of Herman?"

74

"She made no changes. We hadn't reached that point. The will stands as it was written. Herman doesn't get a dime. Of course, he wouldn't anyhow if he killed her. And I understand that it's a very good possiblity."

This is going to kill Alvarez, I thought. Applegate wasn't in Therese's will, so there goes that motive. The poor slob was disappearing slowly as we watched. But, then, he might not have known that, and just killed the old lady because he *thought* he was going to get a lot of money. I stopped myself before inventing any more needless complications.

"Who is in the will, Elliott? We're looking for any kind of lead. Maybe somebody had a red-hot reason for wanting to see Therese dead." I was still a little tense from my encounter with Flora Grimme.

The lawyer glanced at Armand who nodded almost imperceptibly. Then, producing an obviously expensive briefcase which had been squeezed between his chair and the wall, he drew forth a neat package of papers, the will of Therese Colbert.

"I won't try to read all of this document. You know the language. Armand tells me you have a legal education. Pity you didn't do more with it." He smiled sympathetically, and I had to restrain myself from punching him in the mouth.

Sterns cleared his throat while searching through the will for the appropriate passages. What he read aloud was both illuminating and frustrating. Armand, it seems, was the only designated individual heir. He was to receive a generous amount of the estate, mainly in blue-chip investments. However—and this was as much of a shock to Armand as it was to me—the bulk of the estate was left to something called the Max Schwab Foundation of Newport, Kentucky, with offices in Wilmington, Delaware, and Elko, Nevada.

## 17
## *"What is the Schwab Foundation?"*

I GUESS I MUST have looked bug-eyed and incredulous, but I couldn't help it. Holy shit, it didn't have anything to do with *me*. But it was so off-the-wall that I couldn't accept it right away.

"What the hell is the 'Max Schwab Foundation.' Where the hell is Newport, Kentucky? And why does this outfit have offices in Delaware and Nevada?"

Armand sighed. "Please be calm, Pat. My share of the estate will be a million-five or a million-six, give or take a couple of thousand, after taxes. I know nothing about the Schwab Foundation, nor does Elliott. I *do* know about Newport, Kentucky. It is a city on the south bank of the Ohio River, opposite Cincinnati. For many years it was known as a gambler's haven. Casinos and horse books were common, slot machines graced every drug store and ice cream parlor. Everybody knew about it, but everybody was on the payroll. The operators gave generously to charity and nobody even mentioned morality. When the grand jury was in session, the clubs closed down and the slots were removed from retail establishments. Smart people made a lot of money." Armand closed his eyes and dreamed of all the money he could have made in Newport, Kentucky.

He went on: "My aunt—a dancer, remember—used to appear frequently in some of the better places. One—this will amuse you, Riordan—was called the Beverly Hills Country Club. Sadly, it was destroyed in a fire many years ago. I really was much too young to know about these things first hand, but Therese told me some pretty interesting stories when I was growing up and saw her more often.

"What is this Schwab Foundation? I don't know, unless it deals with her philanthropic interests. That, however, I doubt. And the fact that its headquarters is in Newport makes me a bit suspicious. But Wilmington and Elko—that seems bizarre."

The wheels were turning rapidly in my head. Armand's story awoke a dim memory. I *had* heard of that Sin City across the Ohio from Cincinnati. Open gambling and prostitution had flourished there until the early fifties. But why Delaware and Nevada? Hell, Delaware is close to Atlantic City and who doesn't know about Reno and Las Vegas. And why in God's name would Therese Colbert—long-stemmed showgirl, darling of the stage door, investor par excellence—leave the mysterious Schwab Foundation what I guessed had to be several million dollars?

I broke the brief silence that had fallen at the table. "Gentlemen, it looks to me as if we're going to have to find out more about the Schwab Foundation." I turned to the lawyer. "Have you made any contact with it—or them, as the case may be?"

Sterns is pretty cool. "No, Riordan, I haven't. Knowing Therese as well as I do, er, *did,* I believed the best course to take was to bring everything to Armand. That's why I flew out here instead of mailing the stuff. After all, my fee is three per cent of an estate worth five and a half million." The sum I rapidly calculated in my head, with the aid of a small electronic device I carry in my pocket, turned out to be $165,000. "Plus expenses, of course." Air fare to California and back, deluxe accomodations, a round or two of golf. Maybe Sterns was right. Maybe I did waste my legal education.

"So, now what are you gonna do? Do you have an exact address for this spooky Foundation?"

"Only an 800 number which I have not yet called. I wanted to talk with Armand first."

"Then I suggest you call it pretty quick. We've got to get something going here as soon as possible."

Armand glared at me. "Hold on here, Pat. Your part in this deal is finished. You went to Miami. You found my aunt's body. You came back. I paid you. Butt out."

"Sorry, buddy. You got me into this affair, that's true. But I *did* find Therese's body, pretty brutally murdered and in an advanced state of decay. If you think I'm gonna leave it at that, you're crazy."

The scowl on Armand's face told me that he wasn't going to give me any more money. But I have a penchant for pursuing murder cases pro bono. Reiko disapproves and accuses me of mental decay. "You're not too young for Alzheimer's, hawkshaw," she says. "Why don't you see if you can scare up something that pays for a change."

But Reiko wasn't around at The Lodge at Pebble Beach that day. And I bit off a chunk that was probably too big to chew.

I urged the lawyer. "Call 'em. It's an 800 number. Even The Lodge won't make you pay for an 800 number."

Simultaneously we pushed back our chairs from the little table and made for a bank of telephones in the lobby.

Sterns cleared with the hotel operator and dialed the number of the mysterious Schwab Foundation.

After a brief wait, there was an answer. I could tell from the puzzled look on Sterns' face. He listened, but did not speak. Finally, he hung up the phone.

"Well, that's a real kick. Somebody's voice on a machine told me that there was nobody in the office, but if my business was urgent, I could call a number in Sacramento. Whoever it was didn't invite me to leave a message."

"So call Sacramento," I said.

Armand intervened. "Not from The Lodge. Let's go back to my office. I run an account here, but I am not going to pay the telephone charges."

Slowly and silently we left the hotel, got back in our cars and drove into Carmel. I arrived at Armand's restaurant just a shade after he and Sterns got there, and I had a hell of a time finding a place to park. After a couple of turns around the block, I spotted a piece of green curb (30 minutes) and slid in.

When I got to Armand's office, the call had already been made. My client and his aunt's lawyer were sitting staring at each other.

"Well? What's the story? What about the Schwab Foundation?"

Stern looked very unlawyerly at the moment. Rather he looked very tired. I noticed for the first time that he might be considerably older than I had first thought.

"A real person answered, Riordan. Somebody with a flat, almost mechanical voice A professional voice, I think. Probably an answering service. Impossible to tell whether it was male or female. Said it was expecting my call. Said it knew about the death of Therese Colbert. Said it was sorry, but please expedite the probate and send the money to an address in San Francisco. I told it that probate might take nine or ten months or even a year. It said it didn't matter as long as it got the money. She *owed* it to the Foundation, the voice said. It thanked me and hung up."

"So what do you do now?" I was interested but depressed.

"I don't know *what* we can do besides just going through the motions. Armand is the executor—or 'personal representative,' as designated in the will. If you're out of the state of Florida, you can't be an 'executor,' although it's really the same thing. I'll go back to Miami and get the action underway. The tax bite will be large, you know. There are a lot of investments to liquidate. I don't know about Armand, but the other people insist on cash. I think we're stymied."

I felt myself becoming really angry. Some strange "foundation" had emerged from the swamps of Florida to devour a large piece of Therese Colbert's fortune. Some unknown entity had muscled into a murder case and I wasn't going to let it go without a struggle.

"What address? Where in San Francisco?" I know the town pretty well.

Sterns looked at a scribbled note by the phone. "Here, it's on Grant Street. That's what the person said."

"It's Grant *Avenue,* my friend. Everybody knows that. The main street of Chinatown."

"What do you propose to do, Riordan?" said the lawyer.

"Hell, what do you think? I'm gonna go up there and see what's at that address."

"You'll keep in touch, won't you," said Armand. "If you find out anything, you'll tell us, won't you."

"Sure, boss. Now I gotta go."

Sterns shifted uncomfortably. Maybe he knows more than he's telling, I thought.

"Could I pick your brain a minute, Riordan? I'm in the middle of writing a crime novel, and since you deal with these things in your profession, let me bounce this off you. It's about a young attorney who is heavily recruited by a prosperous law firm in the large southern city. They offer him a huge salary and a new car and all sorts of other inducements. But—and this is the twist, you see—the law firm is really in the employ of organized crime, and this innocent young guy soon discovers this and starts working for the FBI. Pretty intriguing, eh?"

I didn't have the heart to tell him.

# 18
## *"You're an* obfuscator, *you know that?"*

ABOUT AN HOUR later I was sitting in my office, staring out the window at the passing traffic on Alvarado Street, wondering (1) what I should do next and (2) why the hell I had got myself into this mess.

My reverie was interrupted by Reiko. "Okay, Riordan, what's the problem? Stop frowning. You look like one of those awful Cabbage Patch dolls."

She had just returned from lunch with Greg Farrell, and I suspected that she had had a couple of glasses of wine, a quantity of the grape which makes her either aggressive or sleepy. She did not appear to be sleepy.

"Honey, can you think of anything about Therese Colbert's house or what was in it that would tell us something about the woman's character?"

I must have looked pitiful.

"Get off it, pal." She *was* aggressive. "You didn't know the old lady and neither did I. It was sad to find her the way we found her, but there was nothing we could do about it. Drop the case, there's not a buck more to be had out of it."

"You know me. I can't accept a dead end. And now most of the lady's money is going to something called the Schwab Foundation, an outfit nobody knows anything about."

"You're sure it's not the stock brokerage? Maybe she was short on a lot of stuff."

"I'm sure it's not the brokerage. They wouldn't let anybody get three or four million dollars short."

She looked thoughtful. "Where did you learn about all this business? Armand tell you?"

"Therese's lawyer's in town. Incidentally, he's the mysterious stranger who visited her house the week before she died. She was going to change the will, but she never got around to it."

"What about this foundation?"

I explained to her what we had found out. The 800 number, the call to Sacramento, the address in San Francisco.

"Chinatown? Why Chinatown? Somebody trying to give this the old Fu Manchu treatment? Trying to make it seem like an Asian plot? I resent that!" She slapped my desk a goodly blow, and I knew it had to sting her hand, but she didn't wince nor cry aloud.

"I don't know, honey. I don't know who's doing what to whom, like the gay guy who goes up to a lesbian's room. Did you ever hear that limerick, kid? I've got a few more. How about, "There was a young fellow from Ghent / Whose . . .""

"Stop! You're an *obfuscator*, you know that?" She had a little trouble with the word, but she got it out. "Spare me your dirty limericks. You know I hate it when you get into a case that's not going to pay anything. But I know when you get your teeth into something like this murder of Armand's aunt, you ain't gonna give up. So what can I do?"

"Go to San Francisco with me. Let me check up on this so-called foundation. Maybe together we can dig something up."

"Hey, wait. This isn't for overnight, is it? Sally is only just now beginning to speak to me. I don't want to get her riled up again."

"No, no, no. We'll go up in the morning, nose around, and come back. No sweat."

"Okay. Suppose we got to the address you've got and find nothing. What do we do than?"

"Little one, I have still got a number of friends in San Francisco. I still have a snitch or two I can tap. I worked for a lot of criminal lawyers up there before I concluded that discretion is the better part of valor and got the hell out before somebody killed me. Now, as you know, I get involved in murder cases only by accident."

She was nodding in assent. "I only wish," she said, "that you'd get into some more glamorous murders. I mean, every murder you've ever had anything to do with has involved a knife or a gun. Well, there was one guy who was shoved off the Bixby Bridge, but he was probably dead before the fall. Why aren't some of the victims you deal with killed with some exotic botanical poison or the venom of an asp or something?" She had a little trouble with "asp," but otherwise her lisp was disappearing. She reads a hell of a lot of mystery books. I try to tell her not to, but she loves 'em. I try to tell her that all mystery writers are dilettantes, frustrated police groupies and the like. She doesn't believe me.

"Look, kid. *Most* murders are committed with knives or guns. Exotic poisons are for Sherlock Holmes or Agatha Christie. In the good old U.S. of A., murder is quick and violent. We're famous for it."

Her eyelids were beginning to get heavy. I helped her to her desk where she laid her head on her folded arms, sighed, and with a beatific smile on her face, went to sleep.

# 19
## *"There's nothing living in there," I said.*


NEXT MORNING I was at the office at eight o'clock, something totally out of character for me. Reiko had arrived before me, though, and was busy straightening out her desk and my desk and the file cabinets and the umbrella stand and everything else.

"Okay, sport," she said, without looking up from her labors, "let's get the show on the road."

I had been up late, watching Jay Leno and trying to decide if he was funny or not, and I was not all that anxious to drive to San Francisco.

"What do you say we do this tomorrow, Reiko-san. As you say, there's no money in this thing for us, so why bother?"

She grabbed my elbow as I was trying to sit down at my desk and jerked me up with remarkable ease. Why do I forget that this is a wiry little baggage with some kind of belt in judo?

"Let's go," she said, firmly.

In a few minutes we were in my disreputable Mercedes two-seater, heading out of town on Highway One. I insisted on driving this time. Our earlier trip to the San Jose airport had been just a wee bit traumatic for me, and I was determined to arrive in San Francisco with no broken bones.

"Let's go all the way on the coast road, Riordan. It's a lot more fun."

"And it takes a couple of hours more, goddamit." I had my mind made up. "I'll compromise. I'll take Seventeen out of Santa Cruz. You can wave at the roller coaster as we go by. We're not out to have fun, kid."

She didn't say more than one or two words the rest of the trip. But I caught her once or twice looking bloody daggers at me out of the corner of her left eye.

We took the loop onto the Junípero Serra Freeway in San Jose and headed for San Francisco. It's a pretty smooth ride at certain times of day, and we'd hit the slow period. It wasn't long before we were at the outskirts of the city local folks used to refer to as The City. Up around San Bruno I had a really eerie feeling, remembering the accident so long ago when Helen was killed. I guess I'll never get that out of my system. One second I was a truly happy married man, the next I was a widower. You don't get over something like that . . . ever.

Reiko spoke: "You're thinking about Helen, aren't you? Maybe we shouldn't have come this way." She squeezed my arm gently and looked at me with real affection in her eyes.

I nodded, and we drove on in silence.

Since the '89 earthquake it isn't as easy to get downtown as it was. There are still many reminders of the earthquake of '89. I still shudder when I remember those pictures of the Bay Bridge, with cars rolling into this humongous hole, and the mess on the freeway in Oakland. Of course, you've always got to be careful of on-ramping and off-ramping. I've never been too sure about the efficiency of the California freeway system. It moves the traffic fast, sure, but lane changes to make a certain exit at fifty miles an hour can be ticklish. And blind on-ramps can be terrifying. You can get where you're going faster, maybe, but the latter part of the journey might be in an ambulance.

We got to Grant Avenue eventually. My old San Francisco driving skills returned, as though I'd never left town. And, believe me, the town *does* take some special skills. There's an old Bill Cosby LP that has a routine that he did about driving in San Francisco. He described hanging on the uphill side of one of the steep Nob Hill streets in a VW bug at a stop sign, unable to see the cross traffic at all, and trying to gun the car out of a 45 degree hang without drifting back three feet into the guy behind him. There wasn't much exaggeration.

I had run out of my usual dumb luck for parking, so I pulled into the garage under Portsmouth Square. The place is dark and threatening on the lower levels, and always smells of urine, but it was the best we could do. Reiko and I walked briskly to the nearest staircase and got out as quickly as we could.

We found the address on Grant pretty easily. The Chinatown portion of the street isn't very long. When Grant crosses over Broadway, it's something else. North Beach, breeding ground of the Beat Generation. The Co-Existence Bagel Shop. A wave of nostalgia hit me. Dim, smoky coffee houses with people who thought they were guitar virtuosos, poetry readings, the pungent smell of grass. Was that really Kerouac I almost ran into early one morning on Third Street? Ah, those were the days. If only I could remember clearly what I did, and *whom* I did, and one single line of the poetry that used to send me into ecstasy. Did I really sit on the next bar stool to Allen Ginsberg?

"What the hell are you dreaming about, Riordan? Let's get moving." Reiko is my anchor to reality. We opened the door at the address we had been given and found a steep stairway. On the left were mail boxes, old and battered and mostly unmarked. One of them, however, bore a stick-on label reading, "Schwab Foundation. Room 8."

Reiko took the stairs at a trot and was not even breathing hard at the top. I moved more slowly, with respect to my aging but efficient cardio-vascular system. We paused in front of a door marked with a brass numeral "8," which was slightly askew.

I knocked. The sound reverberated through the dim, narrow hallway. The silence was deafening.

"There's nothing living in there," I said. "I don't hear breathing. I don't hear heartbeats. It's empty."

Reiko tried the door. "It's locked. Somebody locked it." She was incredulous. On every other occasion during our association, doors have been unlocked or even standing ajar. This one was locked tight.

She got up close to the locked door and was examining it carefully. She traced the door jamb with her finger, then dropped to her knees and examined the sill.

After a long, silent moment—she can stay on her knees longer than any human being I know—she rose, dusted herself off and announced her conclusion: "The damn thing's painted shut. This door has not been opened in months, maybe years. There's nothing in there. But there is a mail box, right? That's all they need."

No doubt about it. It was all they needed, whoever *they* were. But watching a mail box in a dark, cramped entryway in Chinatown was a job I didn't want to undertake.

# 20
## *You never heard of Mission Irish?*

DID I EVER tell you that I fancy myself a connoisseur of Chinese food?

As Reiko and I emerged into the atmosphere of Grant Avenue the wonderful aromas brought back the many strolls I had taken on this narrow thoroughfare, admiring the intricately carved ivory and jade in the shop windows, appraising the duck carcases hanging by the necks in small markets, listening to the click-click-click of mah jong tiles coming from second story windows and the musical Cantonese spoken by passersby.

Well, now I know that people have been slaughtering elephants and other tusked beasts for that ivory, that Szechuan and Hunan cooking is squeezing Cantonese, even though it's hot enough to paralyze the taste buds, and that Chinese chefs often spit in the wok to make sure it's ready.

However, I was suddenly ravenous, so I hurried down a couple of blocks and pushed Reiko up the stairs to Johnny

Kan's. The lunch was marvelous, and I managed to eat everything but the soup with chop sticks.

"Don't you ever talk while you're eating?" said Reiko. "You've just been shoveling it in ever since the food arrived without a word. And you're way ahead of me, even with those round Chinese chopsticks." She insists that chopsticks must be square, in the Japanese fashion. She was eating her lunch with an American fork.

"Sorry, honey. I've been thinking about that mail box."

"What's there to think about a damn mail box?"

"Somebody has to pick up the mail. I can't stay up here and watch the box and neither can you. So I had to think." I pincered a chunk of chicken neatly and brought it gracefully to my lips.

"What do you propose?"

"I dunno. But I've got a couple of ideas. I worked in this town for a lot of years. There must be somebody who owes me. Eat your rice."

There were a lot of people in San Francisco who owed me, some of 'em I am not anxious to see. When I worked for lawyers, I dealt with some pretty dangerous characters. I ticked over some names in my mind.

"Timmy O'Hara!" I said out loud. "He's got to be around somewhere. I did some spade work that saved him a number of years as a guest of the state."

"So, how do we find him?" Reiko knows how to sound skeptical. "This is not Carmel, Riordan, with a population of just over four thousand. This is San Francisco, remember? The City? The city that used to be called Baghdad by the Bay until Baghdad got to be a dirty word."

"I know a cop—if he hasn't retired—and he'll know where to find Timmy." Sergeant Ed McCarthy. Old Mission Irish both of 'em, O'Hara and McCarthy. You never heard of Mission Irish? They were a breed apart. They lived in the Mission District of San Francisco and spoke English with inflections and vowels that sounded more like Brooklyn or

Lower Manhattan. If you were Irish and lived in the Mission during the first half of the twentieth century, you knew everybody and everybody knew you. And if you weren't a cop, you were likely to be a con artist. Or a bit of both.

When we finished lunch, I looked for the nearest phone. Getting hold of McCarthy was surprisingly easy. He was Lieutenant McCarthy now and his voice rattled my eardrum.

"Riordan, you sonofabitch, what happened to you? Somebody told me you moved to Monterey, down there with the elites and the sardines. You got a lot of nerve callin' me after all these years."

"Ed, there ain't any sardines any more. And I'm enjoying myself listening to the scrub jays and living like a gentleman. I need your help. If you can forgive me for interrupting your midday nap."

"I might have known. Okay, Patrick, what's it all about?"

"Have you got any idea where I can find Tim O'Hara?"

"You're goddam right I got an idea. O'Hara is waiting tables at Bardelli's, disguised as an Italian. What time is it? He's probably there now. What do you want him for?"

"Can't tell you now, Lieutenant. I'll keep in touch."

It was easier to walk briskly from Chinatown to Bardelli's on O'Farrell than it was to bail out the car and hunt for a place to park. And, lo and behold, there in the restaurant with a white apron wrapped around his expansive middle, was Tim O'Hara, sporting a large black moustache.

I was able to drag him aside for a brief conference.

"Sure, I'm glad to see you, Pat. But how the hell can I help you?"

I told him about the mail box. No point in going through all the background.

"I'd like to do it for you," he said. "But I'm here five days a week from ten 'til four. Sure I can spend a couple of hours in the morning and the evening. I got a flat out on Green, so it ain't that far. But . . ."

"Please, no more buts. Do you *know* anybody who could

cover the box while you're working. I'm just going to mail a couple of letters to that address and I need to know who shows up to get 'em."

O'Hara was staring over my shoulder at the maitre d' who was bearing down on us. "Yeah, Pat. I think so. Give me your phone number. I'll call you."

I scribbled the number on a matchbook cover and managed to slip it into his hand as he moved swiftly away.

Reiko had been by my side during this brief conversation. "What do you expect from him? Seems a little flaky to me. Will he ever call?"

"Yup. And he'll find out who's emptying that mail box."

# 21
## *"My God, Carlos Vesper!"*

DESPITE MY display of confidence to Reiko, I wasn't sure that O'Hara would come through. After all, it had been quite a few years since I had seen Timmy, and he might have been snowing me just to escape from the maître d'. So I figured I'd have a little time on my hands.

Next day after we got back from San Francisco, I took a deep breath and called Flora Grimme. "Mrs. Grimme? Pat Riordan here. Good as my promise. How about coming out to your place about ten-thirty? Will that interfere with anything?"

She sounded flustered. "Ten-thirty. Let's see. Today is . . . What is today, Mr. Riordan? Tuesday? I suppose it'll be all right. My spiritual advisor is coming in from Carmel Valley at one o'clock. Well, sometimes he comes in time for lunch. Yes . . . I'll see you at ten-thirty. What time is it now?"

The lady is not playing with a full deck, I thought. I told her what time it was and hung up. I wasn't sure that going to her house wasn't hazardous. But I never go back on my word, even if it hurts.

The Grimme estate is one of those huge places on the ocean side of the Seventeen Mile Drive. It was an old home, probably one of the oldest in Pebble Beach. I drove through a gate flanked by two enormous stone pillars and down a winding one-lane road to the house, a dead-ringer for what I had always imagined an English country mansion would look like from reading Evelyn Waugh.

A nondescript man in a tight vest and flowing sleeves let me in the front door.

The foyer was impressive, sort of like the Capitol dome in Washington. The guy in the vest led me into a small room down a short hall and ushered me into the presence of Flora Grimme.

"Well, this is the scene of the crime. Are you satisfied?" she said.

"Do you mean that the strongbox was taken from this room, Flora?"

"I do not know from what secure spot the strongbox was taken. As I told you, I was in the habit of moving it around periodically. How old are you, Riordan?"

She looked at me as if speculating not only on my age, but my body fat and my potency.

"Let's just say I'm over fifty. Are you telling me that you don't know exactly where the strongbox was when it was taken?"

"I don't keep track of those things, sir. I have many social obligations. I'm having a small cocktail party tonight. Would you like to come?"

It was tough keeping a straight face in the presence of this large and dotty female. For the life of me, I couldn't imagine why I'd agreed to come here or why I let myself get involved with this woman. I made a mental note to call George Spelvin, who had given her my name.

"Let's look around the house," I said, hastily.

She stared at me for a moment and swept out of the room. "Follow me," she said.

It took us almost an hour and a half to cover all rooms in the house, the guest house, the apartment over the garage, the garage itself, and the separate structure housing the hot tub. The slope was steep between the Drive and the ocean, and there were many flights of steps to climb, up and down, up and down. When we finished, I was exhausted. We were back in the room where we started.

"Nice place you've got here, Flora. But you can't remember where you hid your strongbox before you discovered that it was missing. Isn't it possible that it isn't missing? That you've just forgotten where you put it?"

"That could not be. Those jewels were worth several hundred thousand dollars. I would certainly be able to find them if they were here." Her eyes were boring holes in me.

Last time she estimated the value of the missing baubles they were worth two million dollars. Flora Grimme was moving slowly toward me and I looked for a possible avenue of escape. Just as she had me pinned up against an overstuffed sofa, the guy in the vest appeared in the door.

"Mr. Mehta is here, madame. Will he have lunch?"

"Of course, Robert. He always has lunch. Well, Riordan, what are you going to do?"

I was thrilled to be able to get the hell out of Flora's house and said the only thing I could think of: "I'll get back to you. Don't worry about a thing."

I didn't know what that meant, but it seemed to placate the lady. I rushed out of the room.

In the hall I almost ran headlong into "Mr. Mehta."

"My God, Carlos Vesper!" I said, hoarsely.

"Jesus Christ, Riordan, don't give me away. I've got a good thing going now. Strictly on the up and up. I no longer sell junk bonds to rich old ladies. I soothe their psyches for a nice retainer."

Vesper, the disappearing stockbroker, who had fled from

the Peninsula into the arms of a female cellist in San Francisco, his skin darkened from many hours in a tanning studio, his head swathed in a silken turban. The man who had complicated my pursuit of the plotters who were planning to attack the Pope—among other nefarious deeds—on his visit in 1987.

"Carlos, I've got to ask you this? Do you know anything about Flora's missing jewelry?"

"Shit, Riordan, keep your voice down. Don't tell her anything. I'll be in touch." He looked panicky.

Flora Grimme appeared in the hall and beckoned the spurious swami to come to her.

I didn't need any help to find the front door.

## 22
## *Reiko arrived late that morning.*

O'HARA CALLED, but it was about ten days later, after I had just about given up on him. I was leaving the office one evening when the phone made its nerve-jangling noise.

"Okay, Riordan. I got something for you. I watched that goddam mailbox mornings and evenings for a week. I hired a Chinese kid to watch it during the day. You owe me, let's see, six hours at a buck and a half an hour for seven days—anyway, make it seventy bucks. For the kid."

I made a rapid calculation in my steel-trap mind and concluded that O'Hara was overcharging me, but no matter.

"So what did you find out? Somebody picked up the mail, right? Some suspicious-looking character had a key to the box and picked up the mail. The stuff I sent was in long brown envelopes, and you or the kid saw some evil type pick 'em up."

"I don't know from evil, Pat, but a couple of days ago, a person picked up the mail. This was a female person, looked about in her middle twenties, long blonde hair in a pony tail. Pulled up in one of those little bitty Mazda convertibles, got the mail and took off. You didn't expect me to follow her, did you? I ain't had a car in fifteen years, Pat."

"Thanks, Timmy. Your check is in the mail," I lied. I'd send him the money, I guess. I'm not that cheap. But the information he'd given me wasn't a hell of a lot of help.

"Just wait a minute, Tim. Can you remember anything else about the girl? Did you get a clean look at her? Anything?"

"She was a good lookin' gal. Pretty face, y'know. Good body. But she moved so fast. I did get the license number on the car, if that'll help."

*If that'll help.* I could have kissed that big dumb Irishman. "May God hold you in the palm of His hand, O'Hara. Give it to me."

I wrote the number down on my note pad, convinced that I had the problem solved. The license number would lead me to the girl, the girl would lead me to the Schwab Foundation, the foundation would lead me to some kind of cockeyed reason why Therese Colbert left most of her estate to an outfit based in Newport, Kentucky, and I'd be home free. I could put the old lady from Miami Shores out of my mind.

With a feeling of mild elation, I left the office and went home. The next day would be soon enough to bug Tony Balestreri for a trace from the motor vehicle department.

When I got back to the house at Sixth and Santa Rita in Carmel, it was getting pretty dark. Dark in Carmel in a residential area when there's no moon is *seriously* dark. I don't usually leave any lights on in the house and I have fallen on my face on occasion trying to navigate to the front door cold sober.

The house was chilly, so I kicked up the thermostat. I've lived here for, let's see, seven years, I think. It belongs to George Spelvin, who lets me live in it rent-free. But, you know, I need a place of my own. And that fifty-two thousand bucks I didn't know I had has me looking for my own little house. Before I could even think about dinner—and I do a lot of thinking about dinner most days—I impulsively called George.

He listened quietly. "Look, kid, I told you I'd sell you *my* house, the one you're livin' in, but you turned me down. I've got to get $400K for it, though. I didn't get where I am without being an astute business man."

George got to where he is by inheriting a considerable fortune, but I didn't say that. "George, the house is nice, but Sally doesn't like it, and if I can find something else, maybe she'll marry me." It was true. Sally found the house to be chilly and uncomfortable.

George sighed. "All right. What do you want from me? Money for the down payment? I guess I could help you. You've helped me enough."

I quickly told him about the money that had appeared miraculously. He seemed surprised, but he couldn't have been more surprised than I was when I found out about it.

"So what *do* you want me to do? You won't buy my house. Bless you. I can sell it to somebody else. Or put it to use in other ways." George used to use the house for amorous assignations until he married his most recent wife. I hoped he wasn't going to start that again, even though it'd probably mean money to me. I was in charge of getting rid of those ladies when George got bored with 'em.

"I've got the down payment. If you could do something to get me a loan, I'd be obliged."

"Riordan, I know for a fact that your income is not going to stand any scrutiny. There isn't a bank in the world that would lend money to you. And there probably isn't a mortgage company that would look at you twice. Tell you what I'll do. *I'll* carry your loan. You pay me as much as you can. It's a hell of a lot better than letting you sponge off me forever. Let me know what you're going to do. Now, get the hell off the line, I'm about to have dinner."

I was shocked. And then I remembered Flora.

"Wait a minute, George. I am truly grateful for what you have proposed, don't get me wrong. But why did you recommend me to Flora Grimme?"

George burst out laughing. "Some case, that one, eh? She's been badgering everybody in Pebble Beach about what she says is the loss of a fortune in jewels. Most of us think she's just nuts, Pat. Rich as hell, but nuts. I thought you'd get a kick out of her. Have a good day." And he was gone.

I couldn't completely forgive George for dumping Flora on me, but I couldn't object too strenuously, either.

You never know. I didn't have a thought in the world of asking George for financial backing. It was his own idea. Damn! I'm a lucky bastard to have people like that. But I didn't like the crack about my sponging off him. That did smart a good bit. And Flo Grimme was still a burden.

But I felt so damn good I walked down to one of the best restaurants in town and ordered without even looking at the prices. Man, that can be daring.

But you're not really interested in my ongoing real estate venture. I've got to tell Sally, though.

Next morning I called Balestreri. "If I asked you real nice, would you be willing to check out a license plate for me? I know you're busy, and you're not supposed to do things like this for a buddy, but I'd sure appreciate it."

The sergeant grunted. "Give me the number, Pat. I know it won't do me any good to object. You'll bug me 'til I do it. Okay, the number?"

I slowly pronounced the letters and numbers on the California plate.

"I'll get back to you." Abruptly, he slammed down the phone.

Reiko arrived late that morning. If she thought I'd ignore the fact, she was dead wrong..

"Nice of you to drop in, kid. Alarm didn't go off, right. Big night last night and the alarm didn't go off. Good to see you anyhow. Sit down and stay awhile."

She turned on me furiously. "You dumb shit, get off my back. You come to work whenever you please, you don't do any of the office work, *I'm* supposed to be your *partner,* and you scold me for being fifteen minutes late." She added a suggestion that I perform an unnatural and physically impossible act, but I'm too much of a gentleman to put it in print.

I was duly chastised. "Sorry, dear. I have some news for you. I thought you might be interested." I told her about O'Hara and his juvenile spy and the gal with the pony tail.

She calmed down. "Isn't this a strange sort of development? Here we are expecting some sort of oriental mystery in the heart of Chinatown, and what we get is some cookie in a Miata."

"O'Hara got the license number. I just fed it to Balestreri. We should hear any—" The phone bleated.

"Riordan, I got your party. The license was issued to a person named Sydney Hammer. Name could be male or female, I didn't ask. Address in Mill Valley." He gave me the specifics.

"Thanks, Tony. And bless you."

"Up yours, Patrick. Goodbye."

Mill Valley, just a bit beyond the Golden Gate Bridge north of San Francisco. Colorful, charming little town on the slopes of Mount Tamalpais. Hell of a place for a conspiracy.

## 23
## *"I'm not with the IRS or the cops."*

THE VOICE on the phone-answering machine was melodious and seductive: "This is Sydney. I'm not home just now. Please leave your number after the beep and I'll call you back. 'Bye."

I stammered out my name and number rapidly and hung up.

Sydney Hammer was a girl. Or she sounded very much like a girl. A girl who was at peace in her world and didn't need to worry about much. I guess I fell a little bit in love with the sound of her voice, but I'm always doing that.

I sat back in my chair and looked at Reiko.

"Honey, I just heard Sydney Hammer's voice and it's female. Sounds like one of those sweet young things who drive pickup trucks recklessly, but dote on their dogs, which are usually dobermans. Her machine says she'll call me back, but I doubt it."

"You're a sap for those young tramps with sexy voices,

101

Riordan. Listen, if that woman was collecting mail from a very suspicious drop, she's up to her ass in this murder mess."

"I dunno, I dunno." It's part of my psyche to think that innocent-looking, innocent-sounding people just can't be involved in nastiness. I make a lot of mistakes because of that feeling.

"Face it. Whether she's just an errand girl or a killer, she's in it. What's your next move?"

I was just about to tell her when the phone rang.

"Mr. Riordan? This is Sydney Hammer. You left a message on my machine. What's it about?"

"Ah, well, gee, thanks for calling back. It's kind of hard to explain. I ought to talk to you in person, you know, like face to face."

"Sounds bad. You sure you don't want to sell me insurance or something?"

"No, ma'am. I'm not a sales person, I'm a private investigator. Uh . . ."

There was a silence on the line. Then:

"Mr. Riordan, I don't think I've done anything wrong. I've never been married and I've always paid my bills on time. I don't *think* I have any outstanding traffic tickets."

"I'm sorry, Sydney. I'm not with the IRS or the cops. And while I do my share of divorce work, this isn't that kind of a deal. But I do need to talk with you."

"Where are you? The 408 area code is all over the map, from San Jose on down the coast. Maybe we could meet somewhere."

"My office is in Monterey. That's is, uh, where I'm calling from. Can we meet somewhere between here and Mill Valley?"

"Now there's a coincidence. I'm coming down there for the weekend with some girls from where I work. I guess I could arrange to see you maybe late Friday or early Saturday."

This is a bit much, I thought. She just *happens* to be coming down here this weekend. She is either very cagey or sublimely ingenuous.

"Let's set a time," I said. "When do you expect to get here?"

"Well, we can't leave 'til after work. So it's going to be kinda late Friday. Let's make it Saturday morning, ten o'clock. Where do I find you?"

I gave her my address on Alvarado Street and we said our goodbyes.

"How do you like that? She's going to meet me here Saturday morning. As innocent as you please."

Reiko frowned. "You are a big chump, pal. You will let this little pony-tailed cutie lead you down the primrose path."

"Where did you get that expression? I haven't heard it in thirty years."

"It's something my mother used to say, when she chose to speak English. I don't know where she got it."

"Well, Sydney's coming here Saturday morning. You're welcome to be present . . . to protect me from attack, maybe. Or perhaps you could give the kid the benefit of the doubt."

She sniffed and left the room. I thought I'd better call Armand.

He sounded suspiciously reluctant to talk. "Hammer, you say. That's a name I've heard before. Therese mentioned it once or twice, years ago. She was always on the road, you know. Hammer. Yeah, I remember."

"You remember what?"

"Therese used to play all the clubs. Especially Vegas and Reno and Tahoe. Places where there was gambling. I guess I didn't tell you Therese was a gambler. In the early fifties, she played those places in Kentucky, y'know. It's pretty dim, but that's where she met a guy named Hammer. But you say this girl is in her twenties? Couldn't be *that* Hammer's child. Some relation, maybe. You say she sounds like sweetness and light personified? Be that as it may, don't turn your back on her, Riordan."

"Why, Armand? My eye-witness in San Francisco says she's a neat little package with a pony tail hairdo."

"It's just something I remember about Hammer. It's foggy right now, but maybe it'll clear up in my mind. He was a real hard guy, as dangerous as they come."

# 24
## *She turned to me with tears in her eyes.*

SATURDAY CAME, and Sydney looked just like she sounded: long, medium-blonde hair, wide blue eyes and a drop-dead body. She sat demurely in my office and I did my level best to look serious.

The young woman (about twenty-seven, I guessed) had arrived promptly at ten. She showed little apprehension. On the contrary, she seemed calm, cool and curious.

"I'm here, Mr. Riordan. Ever since we talked on the phone the other day I have been wondering just what it could be that I could possibly help you with. You really didn't tell me much."

I cleared my throat noisily. "Sydney, you were observed taking mail from a box in a building on Grant Avenue in San Francisco that I happen to know belongs to something called the Schwab Foundation, an outfit that figures prominently in a case I've been working on. Can you tell me what your connection is?"

Sydney grinned widely. "Is that all? You were so terribly mysterious about this whole thing. I could have explained it to you on the telephone. I work in the office of Tierney, Moriarty and DiSalvo, a law firm. One of the things my boss has asked me to do is check that mail box from time to time. Last week there were a couple of envelopes in it that I turned over to my supervisor. That's it."

"That's it? You don't know anything about the Schwab Foundation? You just pick up the mail for a nest of San Francisco lawyers?" I was crushed. Here I thought I had something sort of glamorous going, and this sweet young thing tells me that she's just running an errand. But why Sydney Hammer? Armand recognized the name and connected it with a gambler in Newport, Kentucky. I pulled myself together and tried to retain my dignity.

"Is that all?" she asked. "Can I go now. My girl friends are waiting at the hotel. We want to go to the Carmel beach this morning. Before it gets too crowded."

"Carmel Beach is never crowded, Sydney. It's very wide, the water's very cold, and the surf ain't that great, either. Give me a few more minutes." I was desperate. What could I ask this young woman that would help anything at all? Then I got a quick flash.

"Who's this supervisor? The one you turned over the mail to."

"Her name is Deirdre Hastings. Why do you ask?"

In order to explain why I asked, I had to break down and relate to Sydney pretty much the entire story. Armand, Therese, Herman, Maybelle and Veronica, the whole Miami schtick.

She sat silent for a moment, digesting the bizarre story.

"And you say because my name is Hammer, I'm somehow connected. Because my grandfather operated a casino in Kentucky."

"Your grandfather, Sydney? You freely admit that? Do you think there's something that involves your family?"

106

She rose from her chair and walked to the window overlooking Alvarado Street. As she stared down at the passers by, she talked slowly, soberly:

"It's one of those things that families try to sweep under the rug, Mr. Riordan. My father—who was the best man I ever knew—was the son of Edwin Hammer, my grandfather, and a showgirl who was not his wife. These things we take for granted nowadays, but when my dad was born in the late forties, it was something nobody talked about, even in the family of a gambler operating illegally in Kentucky. Dad grew up in a respectable atmosphere, went to college, and married his childhood sweetheart. I was born in 1965. Dad died in 1972 of a heart attack. My mother lives in a condo in San Mateo. She won't talk about my father because it hurts too much. And she won't talk about my grandfather because she hated his guts."

"The elder Hammer is dead, also? Your grandfather?"

"Yes. He outlived my father by ten years." She turned to me with tears in her eyes. "But why am I pouring out all this stuff to you. I don't *know* you. I'm really alone in the world. My mother doesn't like to see me, so I stay away from her. I don't know any other family." Before she could turn away, I could see the tears flowing down her cheeks.

At this point, Reiko, who had glued her ear to the door of my office shortly after Sydney arrived, threw it open and swept past me to put an arm around the young woman who was by now quite out of control. Sydney was about six inches taller than my partner and the sight of Reiko offering sympathy and compassion to this girl who looked down at her struck me as mildly amusing. However, I did not laugh.

"Okay, Riordan, get out. Go get coffee or something. Don't come back for at least a half hour. While you're at it, bring *me* some coffee. And some for our guest, right?"

Sydney acknowledged Reiko's order with a brief nod and a forced smile. I got out.

When I returned in precisely thirty minutes, the two of

them were chatting like old sorority sisters. Reiko was talking about her family in her animated way, poking the air with her hands and skipping around my desk. Sydney, plainly delighted, was sitting in my chair with a wide smile on her face.

"Am I in the right place?" I asked. "When I left there was high drama here. Do you take cream, Sydney?"

Reiko was actually jubilant. She spilled her coffee on some unpaid bills on my desk as she pirouetted around the room.

"I've got it, Riordan," she said. "It's plain as the nose on your face. Therese was Sydney's grandma. You know, the showgirl who had her father out of wedlock. There's your connection!"

"I already figured that out, honey. The question is why the elaborate cover-up? Why the labyrinth? Who the hell is Deirdre Hastings, and what's her connection? And who killed Therese Colbert and why?"

Sydney turned her pretty blue eyes on me, and just for a moment I thought, "This lady knows a lot more than she's telling."

## 25
## *DiSalvo didn't blink.*

I FREELY ADMIT to the fact that I am not the most intuitive detective in the world. Sometimes I don't think I'm a *real* detective at all. It's a job I fell into, like some guys fall into accounting or retailing. But I've done what I do for thirty-odd years so I must be doing something right. Some years, I admit, were odder than others.

Reiko was on the money about Sydney's relationship to the late lamented Therese Colbert. It all made good sense. But there was something strange going on. Somebody killed Therese before she could change her will. Nobody knows what changes she would have made if she had made any. And the distinguished attorney/author Elliott Sterns was quite sure she *hadn't* made any changes. So I was left to guess whether Therese was killed to keep her from changing the will or maybe because she wouldn't change it. And I was forced to believe that Sydney, for all her innocent appearance, might have had something to do with Therese's death.

While Reiko and Sydney continued to rattle on about the stuff women talk about that men don't understand, I went into the other room and sat in Reiko's damnable Norwegian knee chair. Or is it Danish, I never can remember? It's an instrument of torture that has no back, a tiny seat and a cross-piece to rest the knees on. Great for the posture, Reiko says. A pain in the ass, I say.

I tried to visualize the murder scene as I remembered it. "X," the murderer, is present, discussing whatever with Therese. She tells him (or her) that she's going to change her will to leave a fat package to Herman Applegate. "X" kills her in the Florida room. Alternative scene: "X" tries to get Therese to change the will to include him (or her). Alternative number two: "X" says something like, "You cut out the Schwab Foundation and you're a dead woman." No matter what the question was or what Therese's response was, "X" kills her in the Florida room.

It is my conclusion that there is still a missing piece in the puzzle. Deirdre Hastings? Who the hell is she? Maybe the culprit is one of the partners of Tierney, Moriarty and DiSalvo, employers of Sydney Hammer. Maybe the suave and distinguished Elliott Sterns killed the old lady in a moment of passion. Aw, that's bullshit, Riordan. That guy's never had a passionate moment.

I arose, barely able to bend my knees after five minutes on Reiko's abominable chair, and went back into my own office.

"Sydney," I said, "you are wasting your weekend here. Go on down to your hotel and join your friends. My valued partner and I have to talk this thing through. Have a good time. But stay in touch. Call me before you leave town." I gave her my home phone number.

By this time, the two women had become good friends, each promising the other to maintain contact and exchange pleasantries now and then. Sydney hugged Reiko and left.

"Well, that was quick, " I said. "You two were bosom buddies by the time she left. That's funny, y'know. You don't take to people that quickly. You're usually so, so . . . Japanese. I mean . . . reserved, restrained. You most often take a long time to size people up before you hug 'em."

"She's an innocent lamb, Riordan. I know these things. I go by instinct and I'm never wrong. Remember how you tried to steer me away from Greg? And you were *dead* wrong."

Greg Farrell, Reiko's more or less steady man, is an extraordinarily talented artist who dwells in a hut about halfway to Big Sur. True, I tried to tout her off the man when he showed some interest, but I had no success. She saw in Greg what I had never seen and possibly could never see, knowing the guy as catnip for ladies of all ages. So I had to accept her judgment about Sydney.

"So, if Sydney is an innocent lamb, who the hell is the bad guy?" Yeah, little one, if you're so smart, solve the problem.

"We've got to go back to San Francisco and see this Deirdre something. Talk to the lawyers in the office. Find some sort of connection. Sydney obviously doesn't know anything about the Schwab Foundation."

"Oh, you think that's obvious, do you? And you think we'll discover the secret of Therese's treasure before I get arthritis or need a prostatectomy?"

She stuck her tongue out at me, whirled around and left my office. Damn, she can behave like a five-year-old sometimes. But I guess I was, as usual, being a smartass.

I swiveled my chair to face the window and the day-at-a-time calendar that is forever indicating August 18, 1986. "Reiko," I called, over my shoulder, "you win. I'll pick you up at eight Monday morning and we'll go back to San Francisco."

So we found ourselves late the following Monday morning seated in the austere office of Giuseppe DiSalvo, senior partner of Tierney, Moriarty and DiSalvo. DiSalvo was a tall, spare man, unashamed of his baldness, with piercing eyes and thin lips. As he contemplated the two uncomfortable people before him, he put his finger tips together and rotated his chair a half turn to the right.

"Now, then, Mr. Riordan, what can I do for you?"

I blurt things. I am a blurter. I blurted: "What happened to Moriarty and Tierney? Like it says on the door."

"Dead. They were my father's partners. My father is also dead. The firm name was well established, so we kept it. Again, what can I do for you?"

"We are investigating a murder that occurred in Miami." Now, that sounded pretty silly. It didn't explain anything to Mr. DiSalvo. He looked irritated.

"So?"

"What I mean is, the various trails we've been following have led us to a young woman who works for you named Sydney Hammer."

DiSalvo didn't blink.

"So?"

I could feel the warm flush creeping up my neck and into my cheeks.

"So, we had a little chat with Deirdre Hastings, Miss Hammer's supervisor about a mail drop on Grant Avenue. And it appears that whatever Sydney found in that mail drop was given to her to turn over to you. And we're sort of curious about your connection with the Schwab Foundation."

"Why?"

This guy is too cool, I thought.

"Well, this Schwab Foundation is the main designated beneficiary in the will of the lady who was murdered in Miami, Miss Therese Colbert."

DiSalvo rotated back to his original position without separating his fingertips.

"Mr. Riordan, confidentiality is absolutely inviolable in the practice of law."

"Aw, shit, I know that, counselor. But a woman was brutally murdered. That ought to make some kind of a difference."

DiSalvo separated his fingertips and examined his nails.

"Well, I suppose I could give you the name of the person

who requested that we set up this, uh, arrangement. He's a highly respectable Miami attorney. Elliott Sterns."

That was a blow to the midsection, all right. Sterns had lied to Armand and me. Reiko and I rose to leave.

But I couldn't resist one more question: "Sir, it isn't often you run into somebody named Giuseppe. Were you born in Italy?"

His face was cold, impassive. "My family has lived in San Francisco for five generations. I was christened Joseph. Giuseppe has more distinction. Now, get the hell out of my office."

# 26
## *"She is the ultimate beneficiary of the will."*

STERNS DIDN'T look a bit guilty or sheepish when I confronted him with the information given me by DiSalvo.

"Some things are necessarily confidential, Riordan. Let me be very frank with you . . ."

"That'll be a nice change, counselor," I said, with the heaviest sarcasm I could muster.

"Hear me out." The lawyer was sitting in Armand's office and I was in Armand's chair. "When Therese told me of a son, I was greatly surprised. All during our previous dealings there had been no mention of offspring. The lady came to me one day greatly troubled. In my office, she unburdened herself of something she had kept secret for many years.

"She told me of a love affair in her early life that resulted in pregnancy. She was a strong woman, Riordan, and with high moral principles. She wouldn't consider abortion. It wasn't legal in *any* state in those days. So she carried the child to term and gave birth to her son. The child's father paid all the expenses and kept Therese in luxurious circumstances all during her, uh, confinement."

Confinement? My God, I hadn't heard that expression for a coon's age. To be honest, I haven't heard "a coon's age" for a long time, either. But Sterns had more to say.

"Therese told me about her son when the boy was fourteen or fifteen. He had been accepted by his natural father and given his name, and Therese had maintained contact with the family to know of her son's health and his upbringing. When she told me about him, her purpose was to see that he could be included in her will without giving away her secret. Since the young man was at that time living in California, I called Joe DiSalvo and explained the circumstances. Joe, who had attended to some matters for the boy's father after he moved to California, suggested that we set up a dummy corporation so that money from Therese's estate could be channeled to her son or his heirs upon the occasion of her death. I left the details in Joe's hands. Thus, the Schwab Foundation."

I was far from satisfied. "But if you already knew that the ever-lovin' Schwab Foundation was a front for the heirs, why in hell did you pretend all that innocence?"

Sterns took my question in stride. "Therese was murdered. Brutally. I reasoned that it was somebody who knew about the Schwab Foundation *and* the heirs. Somebody who was furious about not being included in the will, or was trying to intimidate the lady. I didn't want to take a chance on soiling the memory of Therese's son, who is dead, or possibly laying a stigma on somebody else. I came out here in the hope that I might trace down the person or persons who knew about Therese's unfortunate love affair and the child. I thought Armand might be helpful. I hadn't counted on having to deal with you."

"So what are you going to do now? Go back to Miami? We're running into a wall, you know. The will specifies the Schwab Foundation. We find the Schwab Foundation, or a reasonable facsimile thereof. We trace the mail drop to

DiSalvo's office. And he leads us right back to you. This is what you might call a wild goose chase, except that geese never fly in circles. At least, I don't *think* they do."

"I think it's my duty to confer with your Miss Hammer. She is the ultimate beneficiary of the will. Or, according to Joe DiSalvo, the ultimate beneficiary of her father, who is the Schwab Foundation, as specified in the articles of incorporation."

"I'm getting a nasty headache," I said. "Every murder I have had to deal with has given me a nasty headache. And this one is gonna be nastier than all the others put together. Somebody killed Therese Colbert. For a while I thought it was Herman Applegate. Than for another while, I thought it was you. After that, I thought it was some mob character, hired by a sinister organization called the Schwab foundation. Then it could have been Sydney Hammer, God forbid. Or Giuseppe DiSalvo. Somebody stabbed Therese Colbert in her own little house and left her there. Somebody got away. You have to confer with little Sydney. That's all plain and simple. She gets the money. But I have got to find out who killed Therese or I'm gonna go off my rocker."

Sterns looked thoughtful. "I think you'll have a devil of time running the murderer down, Riordan. I can't help you any more, much as I would like to. Right now, I'm wondering how young Sydney will react when I tell her who her grandmother was and why she is getting a lot of money. That's a good news and bad news thing, you know. Your father was a bastard—not in the pejorative sense, of course—but grandma left you a nice chunk of money."

He left the office, shaking his head. I sat uncomfortably at Armand's desk, drumming my fingers on his spotless blotter. I wondered idly why they still put blotters on desks when nobody ever uses 'em. Then Armand returned from whatever errand he had been on and was surprised, and a little irked, to find me in his place.

"What have you found out, Pat? I know you went to San

Francisco and there was something about a mailbox. You talked with somebody—a young girl—and then you made another trip. I paid you. Now, report."

"You paid me to go to Miami and find out what happened to your aunt. I did that. I don't owe you a damn thing. But I'll tell you anyhow." And I brought him up to date.

He sat down heavily across the desk while I remained in his chair. "A son. An illegitimate son. And a granddaughter who works in San Francisco. This is really a shock, Pat. I thought I enjoyed Therese's absolute confidence. She would have told me. Why didn't she? She was my favorite aunt."

"Remember what Maybelle and Veronica said? About a 'relative in California'? Or 'somebody that was just like a relative'? Not you, Armand. Not necessarily any of your known family. But now we've got a whole new set of relatives, haven't we? I think I'll call sweet little Sydney Hammer and see if she can enlighten me."

# 27

# *"Please don't give me away, Riordan."*

THE LOOK on Reiko's face when I got back to the office was one of wonder. It was something between a smile and a smirk, and I could tell she was bursting to tell me something of enormous import.

She whispered: "Guess who's in your office, Patrick. Nah, you'll never guess. I hardly recognized him. He looks like something out of *Jewel in the Crown*. Dark skin, turban . . ."

"Carlos Vesper," I said. "Yeah, I was expecting him. Not so soon, maybe. But I knew he'd be coming here."

Her mouth opened but nothing came out for a few seconds. "You know? How could you know? What . . . ?"

"The woman from Pebble Beach. You know, the one who came to me about stolen gems. He's her 'spiritual advisor,' honey. I ran into him at her house. Carlos asked me not to give him away. He'd explain everything. I can hardly wait."

Vesper was slumped in my guest chair with his chin on his

chest. I walked around him to my desk, being careful not to disturb him. He did not look up.

Still staring at the floor, he spoke: "Okay, Riordan, when I left the Peninsula, I really intended never to come back. There wasn't any way I could resume a normal life around here. The people I sold those rotten securities to, they'd kill me, or at least have me arrested. But I liked it so much here. I wanted to come back. Down in L.A. where I wound up, I couldn't make a living. Couldn't get a job and wouldn't work in the fast-food business. But I read the *Times* every day, and one day there was this ad from some guy in Ventura who said that he was a 'psychic counselor,' and he'd come to your house to help you solve your problems.

"Jesus Christ, I said to myself, what a great racket. I've always had a soothing effect on older ladies. Why not give myself a new persona and become a psychic counselor. Women go for the exotic, y'know, so I picked a name and got this suntan. Costume shop in Hollywood made the turban. The name I got from that symphony conductor, you know, the Indian guy, *India* Indian, I mean."

"You named yourself after Zuban Mehta? Carlos, you are certifiable. You promised me you'd go straight and pay me the money I lent you to get away from here. So you turn up in Pebble Beach as spiritual advisor to a nutty lady who has dragged me in to look for her stolen jewelry. Have you no shame, man? By the way, what's the difference between a psychic counselor and a spiritual advisor?"

"There isn't any. But no matter. Please don't give me away, Riordan."

"Did you take the lady's jewels, Carlos? Tell me now, and we'll save a lot of time."

"No!" he said vehemently. "Well, not exactly." He had finally looked up from the floor and was trying to meet my eyes.

"This is Riordan, fella. Tell me the truth."

He sighed mightily. "You aren't the first guy to discover I'm back in town. Another man, one of the people I sold those lousy bonds to, he spotted me before I was here a week. I thought the deep tan was enough. Goddammit, I shoulda grown a beard. Passed for a Sikh. Anyway, the guy said he'd keep it quiet if I got his money back. Well, Flora is paying me pretty well, and I've got a couple of other ladies on the string. But I just didn't have the kind of money the guy wanted. So I borrowed Flora's jewels."

"What the hell do you mean by that? You borrowed them? Holy shit, Carlos, what did you expect to do with them? That kind of ice is impossible to fence around here. And God knows you can't sell the stuff."

He was crestfallen. "I know, I know. I guess I just wasn't thinking, Riordan. I was scared. I owe this guy like twenty thousand dollars, and borrowing the jewelry was the only way I could think to get it. It was a dumb stunt."

"You've still got the stuff?" I asked. You've got to get it back to Flora's house. Maybe I can help you with that."

"Yeah, but what am I going to do about this clown who wants the twenty thousand? I'm never going to find that kind of money."

"Get a job. Go to work. Make a deal with the guy. You know, so much a month you'll pay him. I sure as hell haven't got it to lend you."

Vesper was defeated and he knew it. "Okay, Pat. Next time I'm at Flora's I'll sneak the strongbox in somehow."

"Put it where I can find it. Then I'm off the hook with the lady, and maybe you can borrow the twenty thousand from her. She'll spend that much on clothes in the next month."

Carlos was genuinely grateful, and promised to conceal the strongbox behind the drapes in the small room where Flora had received me.

I slapped him on the back as he went out of my office, slightly dislodging his turban, revealing a definite line of white flesh a couple of inches above his eyebrows. The tanning parlor treatment hadn't been enough, I guessed.

After showing the "advisor" out of the office, I turned to hear the phone ringing.

Reiko looked up after answering it. "It's for you," she said. "Sounds like a lady with a bad case of laryngitis."

# 28
## *Her face was handsome, but not beautiful.*

THE VOICE on the phone was indeed low-pitched and husky.

"This is Martha Hammer. I'm Sydney's mother. Can we arrange to meet somewhere very soon?"

I was not exactly bowled over by the call from the lady in San Mateo, but it was a bit of a surprise.

"Sure, Mrs. Hammer, you name it." I had been about to call Sydney the morning after I had that frank (for a lawyer anyhow) discussion with Sterns. Actually, I had been in the act of reaching for the phone when it bleated.

"Let's choose a neutral site, Mr. Riordan. Can you make it for lunch in Palo Alto?" She named a prominent Chinese restaurant.

"Yeah, I'll be there. How will I know you?"

"I'm known at that restaurant. Just ask for me when you arrive. Shall we say half past noon?"

"Sounds okay. But why can't you enlighten me on the

phone? Is what you want to discuss so terrible that you have to lure me into a Chinese restaurant?"

She laughed, sounding a lot like Lauren Bacall. "Not terrible, Mr. Riordan. But of considerable importance. That is, if you are still interested in finding the murderer of Therese Colbert." And she hung up.

The lady sounded formidable. And she invited me to lunch at one of the San Francisco Peninsula's very best Chinese restaurants. Even if it turned out to be nothing at all, I couldn't refuse the opportunity. Besides, I was curious to know what kind of woman Sydney's mother was. It has always been hard for me to understand mamas who isolate themselves from their children. The biological phenomenon of motherhood doesn't necessarily create an emotional bond between mother and child. But it should count for something. At least, that's how I feel.

I fished my little drugstore glasses out of my shirt pocket and looked at my watch. A little after nine-thirty. At best, the trip from Monterey to Palo Alto ought to take less than two hours. But a number of road projects were underway on Highway 101, and I could never be sure how long it would take me to go anywhere.

Reiko was noodling on her computer as I passed through her area. "I'm off to Palo Alto, kid. Got a call from Sydney Hammer's mother."

"I heard," she said, without looking up. "You just can't resist a free Chinese meal, can you?"

There is nothing I can do about Reiko's eavesdropping on my telephone calls. I ceased to try long ago.

"I'll be back late in the afternoon sometime. Please feel free to close the office and go home whenever you choose."

She turned a fierce glare on me. "I go and come as I please, *partner*." Then she smiled brightly. "Drive carefully."

I shrugged and departed.

The trip was less than memorable. There were no serious traffic delays and I reached Palo Alto about eleven-thirty, driving at just a pinch more than the speed limit. This is a dangerous thing to do on California freeways. Big semis pass you doing eighty-five. And I've never seen a semi pulled over by a highway patrol car, have you?

Since I had a little time to kill, I drove over to the Stanford campus, which features a tower affectionately referred to as Herbert Hoover's Last Erection. Stanford is not in Palo Alto, you know. It's just Stanford, California, an entity unto itself. But it's a beautiful campus. I parked and watched the students strolling on a sunny day, wishing for just a little while that I could recapture some of that youthful confidence. I really never had a chance. Korea happened when I was about to go to college, and when I came back, I wasn't—couldn't be—Joe Cool. Water over the dam . . . or under the bridge, I forget just how that one goes.

I reached the restaurant at the appointed hour and, as per instructions, asked for Mrs. Hammer. A smiling young woman in one of those oriental split skirts led me to a table in a secluded corner.

Martha Hammer was a very impressive woman. She rose from her chair to greet me, and her handshake was firm and vigorous. "Pleae sit down, Mr. Riordan," she said.

Mrs. Hammer was about five-eight, one-forty-five or -fifty, give or take a few ounces. In her middle to late forties. More than just an aerobic exerciser, I thought, probably did weight work a couple of times a week. In good shape, this woman. So was the young Chinese woman in the split skirt, I thought, as I watched her walk away. But not nearly so muscular as Martha.

Mrs. Hammer's brown hair was streaked with natural gray and hung to her shoulders. She was wearing an expensive tailored suit. I couldn't see her feet, but I guessed sensible shoes. Her face was handsome, but not beautiful. Sydney must have had her exquisite features from her father. Or her grandmother whom I had seen only in death.

We talked a bit about the weather and studied the menu.

After we ordered (I confess I held back a little), she opened another avenue of conversation.

"You're wondering what interest I have in the death of Therese Colbert, aren't you?"

"It had crossed my mind, as long ask you've asked."

She looked me straight in the eyes. "My husband confessed to me long ago that he knew about his real mother. I'm not sure how he found out. His father was an uncommunicative man, an unfeeling man. He didn't want his son to marry me. Even offered to buy me off. But we ran off to Reno and that was that. And when Sydney arrived, all seemed to be well."

Martha Hammer paused to take a sip of tea. "The lawyer DiSalvo entered into a sort of conspiracy with my father-in-law and Therese Colbert to make sure that I was bypassed by Therese's will. I was not supposed to know about the arrangement, but DiSalvo, who owed me a favor or two, called me and warned me about it. They set up that phony Schwab Foundation that would funnel all of Therese's money to my husband, if he had lived, or to Sydney, if he had not. When my husband died, I was left with very little. Fortunately, I am not a stupid woman. I have managed to carve out a successful career in business. I'm financially independent. But I have always resented being ignored by Edwin Hammer and cut off by my husband, Bruce Hammer, and in recent years, by Sydney. That's why I flew back to Miami to pay a visit to Therese Colbert, a fact which you would ultimately have discovered, I'm sure. But I did not kill her, even though I made certain . . . threats."

The relative in California. Had to be Martha. She's telling me that she flew all the way across the country to talk to—to "threaten" —Therese Colbert. But, no ma'am, she didn't kill Therese. But that's what they all say.

A whole lot of thoughts came crashing together in my head like runaway cars in a freight yard. It was too much to handle all at once. I needed a break for my brain to cool.

Fortunately, the food arrived at just about the right time. And, confused or not, I enjoy eating Chinese food.

The rest of our conversation that day added up to small talk. Martha had got something off her formidable chest, and I got a free meal. She waved me away haughtily when I started to fumble for my wallet, and we parted with another brisk handshake.

I watched Martha Hammer get into a silver Mercedes sedan and drive away. I got into my abused little two-seater and took off in the opposite direction.

All the way to Monterey, I tried to fit the pieces of the puzzle together. Damn, the pieces wouldn't go together . . . and there was too much blue sky.

## 29
## "You're going to need a bed, for God's sake."

GEORGE SPELVIN called me the next day.

"Pat, I ran into an old friend of mine at The Lodge yesterday afternoon. She told me that her mother had passed away. I expressed my sympathy, even though I had never met the mother. But that's not why I called. No reason you should care about her mother, either. It's just that the woman said her mom had a little house down on Santa Fe that ought to be just about right for you. It'll take all your fifty thousand, but I'll lend you the rest. Go see it."

He gave me careful instructions about finding the house. In Carmel it is absolutely necessary to give specific instructions. The streets run every which way, and there are no numbers on the houses. Everybody gets lost once in a while, even Federal Express, although there is only one driver covering the whole town and he's given special training in how to find who on what obscure two-block street.

Anyhow, I went down to see the house. It's a neat little

place in a quiet spot, two bedrooms, two baths, couple of decks. I stayed quite a while, wandering around the house and the neighborhood. When I got back to the office, I called George back.

"Okay. Looks good. What do I do next?"

He gave me the name of a real estate agent with a very old, established firm in town. "They aren't the listing agency, but I've got friends there. They'll treat you right."

Anybody who has gone through a real estate transaction knows, probably as well as I, what a pain in the ass it can be. But it came to pass, as the Bible says, that the deal went through, and with George's endorsement and money, the house became mine. The trouble was, nearly all the furniture in the other house was George's.

At this point Reiko took over. "You're going to need a bed, for God's sake. That's the minimum. And some stuff for the living room. Haven't you got *any* money?"

I consulted my bank account. After my down payment and closing costs, I had a couple of thousand dollars left.

"Okay," said my partner, "that'll buy the bed, a couch, and a chair. Maybe a few dishes. Some stainless flatware." Her voice trailed away to a whisper. "Maybe I can come up with something. Mother's got a lot of my stuff up in San Jose. I'll call her."

"I've got my own TV, kid. George didn't have one. He used that house to entertain women, and they sure as hell didn't watch TV. And the stereo is mine." I stopped short. That was it. I owned nothing else in the house I had lived in for seven years.

I'll skip the cleaning and moving. I was exhausted making trips back and forth just with my clothes and my TV and my stereo. I completely forgot about requesting service from the Pacific Gas & Electric Company and slept in a dark, unheated house for three days. Then Reiko reminded me to have a phone put in and the TV cable activated. On the Monterey Peninsula, you just don't get much TV unless you have a big dish or a cable attachment. In George's house I took everything for granted. Now I was on my own, and I had a hell of a lot to learn.

After about a week, George called: "All right, how are you going to pay me? Make it easy on yourself. You owe me about a quarter of a mill. Grand a month sound okay?"

A thousand dollars a month. Cheap for Carmel, I know. But twelve thousand dollars a year. Holy shit! Without interest even it would take me more than twenty years, unless I won the lottery. Which is absolutely ridiculous.

I sat on my new couch and turned on my old TV. It didn't matter what was on the tube. I wasn't watching. It's a hell of a responsibility, owning a house. But maybe Sally will marry me now.

Meanwhile.

All during my fearless real estate venture, I was also having to cope with the nagging problem of who killed Therese Colbert. We had reached a kind of lull in the action. My focus was on the Hammer family, although I really didn't like the idea of little Sydney being the culprit. She seemed like such an innocent lamb. But, hell, it's always the one you least suspect that turns out to be the murderer, right? Unless it's the butler. But who has a butler these days? Not even George Spelvin (pseudonym), my benefactor.

I had just about forgotten about the two ladies from Miami. A call to the Doubletree told me that they were still there, although not in their room. My God, they'd been in town almost two weeks, staying at one of the better hotels. And Maybelle Carothers had told me that she and all her crowd had envied Therese, who had a good deal more money than any of the others. Well, Maybelle and Veronica Small had been having the time of their lives, taking in all the attractions on the Peninsula, eating in the best restaurants, and living high on the proverbial swine.

When I finally got Maybelle on the phone and suggested that she was having quite a nice vacation, her answer was: "Well, why the hell not? Victoria and me are pretty old, Riordan, older than Therese, as a matter of fact. Both of us had some money in the bank. And you can't take it with you, can you? Never thought we'd ever get to California. Didn't even want to, really. So we shoot the whole bankroll. Who cares?"

I can't argue with that. *Carpe diem,* I always say.

"Maybelle, Victoria told me that some tall gentleman in a suit visited Therese's house a week or so before she died. Could there possibly have been *two* tall gentlemen who looked somewhat alike? I mean is she absolutely sure that it was the same guy each time?"

I listened as Maybelle turned to her companion and asked: "Vicky, this is that Riordan guy. Could you maybe have seen two different men visit Therese's house?"

Victoria's answer was unintelligible to me. All I could hear was Maybelle breathing heavily and saying, "Uh-huh, uh-huh." Then, having heard Victoria out, she blasted into my ear once more: "She says it could've been. Whatever that means. You see, Victoria watches out of a side window, and it's a matter of about half a block to Therese's house. And her eyes aren't that good, y'know. What's that, honey? Oh, she says the man was wearing a dark suit. Coulda been another man wearing a dark suit."

I was getting edgy. "Was he driving? If he was, what kind of car was he in? Same car every time?"

Maybelle apparently clapped her hand over the mouthpiece of the telephone, causing my eardrum to vibrate intensely. When she came back on, she said: "Vicky isn't sure. There was a car, yes. Same car or not, she doesn't know."

I sighed. "I'm just trying to find out if it was Therese's lawyer every time, or somebody else."

"You mean that Sterns fellow? Why didn't you say so? Vicky, he thinks it was that lawyer Sterns." I could hear a shrill little cry in the background. "What ever gave you that idea, Riordan. Vicky and me, we know Sterns. We both had him draw up our wills. The man Victoria saw at Therese's door was definitely not Elliott Sterns."

130

## 30
## *"I don't really spy on people,*
## *Mr. Riordan."*

FOR A VERY SHORT while I managed to forget about
Therese Colbert's murder. The only thing that was really
gnawing on me was the fact that Herman Applegate was still
stashed at the Mission Inn, running up a bill. Armand wasn't
going to be very happy when it came time to pay the tab.

Getting used to a new house is a chore, believe me. I wor-
ried about the house being on the side of a hill. Would the
first hard rain wash me down into the house that sits twenty
feet below me? Would the decks stand up on those spindly
supports? What was causing that *clunk* in the living room
floor when I stepped on a certain spot? How was the wiring?
Would I see my fifty thousand dollars go up in smoke, along
with George's investment in me?

You've got to believe that usually I am not a panicky type
of guy. But this was *my* house, not somebody else's. This was
the first time I had ever lived in a place of my own. All those
ratty little apartments in San Francisco that I lived in after

Helen was killed were behind me. George's house at Sixth and Santa Rita had been a wonderful change for me. But now—hell, I am responsible for a whole goddam house.

Reiko and her mother did most of the furnishing. Mama-san came down from San Jose riding shotgun in a pickup that was stuffed with all kinds of things. And I needed them all.

"Okay," said Reiko. "Consider all this a loan without obligation. It's still mine, see, but I'm not using it, so you can. Well, some of it is mama's, but she doesn't need it either." Reiko's mother, who has never smiled at me, wouldn't even look me in the eyes. She departed silently with the pickup driver, a Caucasian male wearing a baseball cap. He was as silent as mama-san, with long hair and a beard that all but hid his features. The pickup left a stinking trail of exhaust as it raced up the hill towards Highway One.

I managed not to think of Therese's murder for a few days. There were routine things to do in my office, the usual investigative tasks that paid the bills. But it all came back to me one morning a couple of days after I had moved when Victoria and Maybelle showed up in my office.

"Glad we came, Riordan. Not so's we could tell what we know about Therese, but because this is just a real great place to visit. I don't know why in the world we wound up in Miami. It's hot and damp and you could get blown away by a hurricane. Of course, you've got those pesky earthquakes here. But nothin' has happened so far, has it? I mean while we've been here. We're thinkin' about goin' down to Los Angeles. They have 'em down there, don't they?"

"Nothing while you were here, Maybelle. Oh, there might have been a little one while you were asleep. Or two or three little ones during the day. Earthquakes are happening all the time here, you know. Thousands of 'em. But they're little bitty ones that just show up on seismograph machines. When you actually *feel* one, it's usually a pretty good shake."

"Vicky has something to tell you, Riordan. About the visitors at Therese's house. Tell him, Vicky."

The small, silent woman looked shyly up at Maybelle and then directly at me. "I don't really spy on people, Mr. Riordan. That is, I don't just sit there all day staring out at the neighborhood. The truth is, the neighborhood has changed a lot since I bought my house. Lots of foreigners have moved in. Cubans, Haitians. You know."

"I'm not sure I do, Victoria. But I forgive you for noticing what happens on your block, if that's any help. What is it you have to tell me?"

"There were two different men who came to Therese's house the week before she was found dead. I told you that. One of them was Mr. Sterns, the lawyer. The other was a tall, gray-haired man who didn't stay very long. But it seems to me there was somebody else. It's real hazy, but somebody else was there just a few days before the cops came. I guess you called them, didn't you? Maybe it'll come to me later. Maybe it won't."

I thanked the two ladies for their visit and keeping me in mind. I had to submit to a bone-crushing hug from Maybelle, but only a gentle handshake from Victoria. I ushered the women to the door, warned them about the steep stairs, and bade them Godspeed. If they had to go to L.A. it was up to them. They'd probably wind up on "Wheel of Fortune" and win a lot of money.

Reiko, who had been down in the Italian delicatessen getting coffee, saw them emerge into Alvarado Street and dashed up the dark staircase, splashing cafe au lait most of the way.

"What's up, Pat? What did those two old girls want? I know. One of 'em has fallen in love with you and came to carry you off to Miami, right? Nope, that can't be it. I hate to say this, but you're too young for either one of them. So—what was it all about?"

"They just told me something I already knew. Victoria couldn't quite remember what it was, but it caused my synapses to crackle briskly. Sydney Hammer's mama was probably pulling a con on me."

## 31
## *"It's sort of like a raccoon with a long nose."*

MY OLD FRIEND the Spiritual Advisor called me again.

"Riordan, I can only talk a minute," he said. His voice was a hoarse whisper, barely audible.

"What's up, Carlos?" I asked. "Are you hiding in a telephone booth? Have the police caught up with you? Surely you're not going back to peddling junk bonds, are you? You know what happened to Keating. And he was supposed to be respectable. You've never been respectable, Carlos, even though you had a Lamborghini Countach and a house in Skyline Forest. Talk to me."

"I've done it. I've managed to return Flora's strongbox. It's in the closet in her bedroom, just around to the right as you open the door. Covered it with an old quilt. You'll be able to find it."

"How'd you do it?"

"It was my regular visiting day, y'know. I told Flora I had a

134

recurrence of an old tropical fever on me and I felt faint. Told her there wasn't anything that would help me but some herbal stuff from a health food store in Pacific Grove. She was eager to put me down on her bed and dash out for the stuff. Pretty clever, huh? When she was gone, I went to my car, got the box, and stuffed it into her closet. Case closed, right?"

"Although it was very thoughtful of you, Carlos, I am at a loss as to how I can discover the strongbox. What do I do? Pretend that I had just remembered an important clue that I picked up when I first visited her? Come out there with a special divining rod adjusted for jewelry?"

"You figure it out, Riordan. I got the stuff back. You've got to find it for Flora."

"Okay. I'll figure out a way. I'm totally blank on how, but I'll figure it out."

"One other thing," he was still whispering, "be careful. The old woman keeps a pet coati mundi in her bedroom. Damn thing bites, too. But he's usually under the bed."

"A *what?*"

"A coati mundi. It's sort of like a raccoon with a long nose. Doesn't have the funny mask, but it bites. Watch yourself." Carlos paused a moment. "Jesus, there she is now. Gotta go!" And he hung up.

I sat there stupid for a few seconds with the phone still plastered to my ear until the damn thing started that raucous sound it makes when the other party has broken the connection.

Reiko came into my office. "What was that all about, pal?" She had been listening again. "You really think that guy would tell you the truth? Not about the strongbox, about the—what was it—a 'cooty Monday'?"

"Yes, dear, I think that this is just the kind of situation that only Carlos can get into. He's a sort of genius, I truly believe. If there are more colorful ways of getting into trouble, Carlos will find them. And I know what a coati mundi is. It's a South American animal, occasionally found in the southwestern

United States, that nobody, but *nobody* ever keeps for a pet. Except people like Flora Grimme. I would not be at all surprised to learn that she also has a dungeon in her basement full of whips and chains and the like. I fear for poor Carlos. It may not go well with him if she ever learns his true identity."

"What are you going to do?" she asked.

"I am going to sit here and contemplate the situation. I may sit here and contemplate all day. I may contemplate for a week. Carlos has done me one small favor, though. He has driven from my mind—albeit temporarily—the case of Armand's aunt."

She went out, laughing hysterically.

## 32
## *And his scent was growing stronger.*

I T WASN'T more than an hour later that I got a call from Herman Applegate asking me to meet him at his hotel.

"Mr. Riordan, I haven't been altogether straight with you, and there are some things you ought to know."

"Herman, you are only out of jail by the grace of Tony Balestreri and me. We don't think you killed Therese, and neither do the Metro-Dade police . . . now. At least, I *think* Lieutenant Alvarez is convinced. Hard to know just what he thinks. If you have information that you withheld from us, it could go badly for you. I have to warn you in advance—even though I'm not a cop—that anything you say to me now might work against you in court. Sure you don't want a lawyer?"

"I thought you were a lawyer."

"Well, yeah, I am . . . sort of. But I don't practice law and I sure as hell can't defend you." I was trying for some reason to get out of seeing this guy again, although I can't for the life of me tell why. I gave it up.

"Okay, Herman. It'll take me about forty-five minutes to get cleaned up here and make it over to your place. See you", I squinted at my watch, "about eleven-thirty."

All I could think of during the drive over to Carmel was, "What the hell could this guy have to tell me?" I had been chasing my tail for weeks trying to pin down just who killed Therese Colbert and why. And now Herman Applegate, the original red-handed suspect, was going to impart some information he had held back.

Y'know, often I have suspected that I look like an easy mark for a con. Slightly beyond middle-age, slightly overweight. Blue-eyed and innocent-looking. Hair gray and thinning inexorably on top. Your ideal bait for the trickster. But Herman Applegate was not going to put anything over on me, no sir.

The man looked even shabbier and seedier than when I had first met him. He had apparently not brought a change of clothes when he arrived from Miami, and his bad brown suit looked like he had slept in it. From his person there wafted the faint aroma of decay or mildew or something. Herman's sad eyes had developed huge pouches, and his skin was the color of Grey Poupon. He was a mess.

We walked into the coffee shop of his hotel and sat on a banquette at a table in a far corner.

"First, you gotta understand that I really loved Therese. Not your mad, passionate kind of love, for God's sake. She didn't want any physical stuff and I'm kind of over the hill in that department, too. No, it was something else, something that I had honestly never felt before. Therese could be real nasty, *real* nasty. But she could also be the kindest, gentlest person in the world. She was awful good to me. Why, I don't know. She'd had a lot of men friends, most of 'em younger and better lookin' and a hell of a lot richer. But she just sort of took to me. She depended on me."

Applegate's sad eyes filled with tears and he sniffed loudly as he ran his right index finger under his nose. He picked up a paper napkin from the table and wiped his eyes. He really hadn't looked at me when he spoke, focusing on something in the middle distance over my left shoulder.

"I been beatin' around the bush, I guess. Let's get to it. Therese and me were talkin' about getting married for a couple of weeks when I got this telephone call from this woman in California. How she got my number—how she even knew about me—I just can't figure. But she said she was some kind of kin to Therese and wanted to know just what was goin' on."

"Did she identify herself? What name did she give?"

"She wouldn't say. I asked her a couple of times, but she wouldn't tell me her name."

"Did she sound like a young woman? An old woman? Something in between?"

"Hard to tell on long distance, y'know what I mean? The sound was kinda scratchy. But what she said shook me up. When I told her that Therese and me were planning to get married, she didn't say anything for a long time. I thought she'd hung up. But just before I put the phone down, she said, 'I'd better come there. You'll hear from me.' "

I sighed. "Is that all? All you had to tell me is that you got this phone call from California from a woman who wouldn't identify herself and said she'd be coming to Miami? Herman, I am sorry but it ain't any help at all."

My God, I thought, I'm beginning to sound like Lord Peter Wimsey. Believe me, I usually don't talk like that. I've got a completely legitimate Jesuit bachelor's degree and a law diploma from a very distinguished school in San Francisco. I have always been acutely conscious of the necessity to use correct English, whatever that is these days. But Herman Applegate was a frustrating creature, and I felt cheated some-how when all he had to tell me was that Martha Hammer had ferreted him out and telephoned him.

Martha Hammer? Of course that was the first name that came to mind while Herman was describing his telephone call. But was it Martha? Herman was unclear on whether he was talking to a young woman or an older one. He was sure the call was from California, though. Why? Was it a person-to-person operator assisted call?

"No, Mr. Riordan," he said when I asked him, "she just said 'I'm calling from California' when she came on."

Herman looked at me with those bloodshot eyes. There were drying tear tracks on his cheeks. His mouth hung open, revealing an irregular, coffee-stained line of teeth. At that moment I thought he was possibly the homeliest man I had ever sat next to. And his scent was growing stronger. I didn't want to cause the guy any more pain, but I moved slowly away from him to breathe some fresher air.

"Do you remember anything else about the call, Herman? Any details at all?"

He frowned and picked up a spoon. Dislodging a bit of dried food from it with a fingernail, he slowly shook his head. And then, something caused his eyes almost to light up.

"She said something about a swab that I didn't understand. I guess it was a swab, like a Q-tip, y'know. I couldn't make any sense out of it. Did I know anything about a swab? That's what she asked."

"Schwab, Herman, Schwab. It's a name. Of German extraction. Lots of people named Schwab. That's the word she used, wasn't it?"

His face cleared. He looked almost happy. "Yeah. I guess it was."

Well, maybe there was something new on the table after all. Maybe the caller wasn't Martha. Sydney? I didn't want to think so. Somebody else? Somebody in Florida, maybe? Somebody who knew about the Schwab Foundation gimmick, for sure. Maybe in the office of Tierney, Moriarty and DiSalvo? Maybe somebody working for Elliott Sterns? Or maybe somebody who lived on that Miami Shores block of NW 92nd Street.

## 33
## *"Sydney's a girl, Herman."*

I WASN'T SURE THAT Applegate's caller had been Martha Hammer, even though that was the most likely conclusion. It seemed so out of character for Martha to call the man just to threaten him. As a matter of fact, whoever the caller was *didn't* threaten him. She (if it was indeed a "she") simply told him that she would be coming to Miami.

"Well, Herman, did she ever show up? Did she come knocking on your door? Did she confront you with a forty-four magnum? What?"

"That was all I ever heard from her, Mister Riordan. That one phone call. In a couple of days I just dismissed the call. Forgot about it. Until now."

I sighed. "Herman, do you remember Therese's ever mentioning Sydney Hammer?"

"No. Who's that? An old boy friend or something?"

"Sydney's a girl, Herman. And she just happens to be Therese's granddaughter. Never heard of her, huh?"

Applegate was thunderstruck. "Granddaughter? Therese told me she'd never been married. How could she have a granddaughter?"

"I hate to break this to you, my friend, but it is not necessary to be married to have a child. In Therese's case there was a romantic involvement with a night club owner in a place called Newport, Kentucky, which resulted in a pregnancy. She was too proud to go to an illegal abortionist, so she carried the child to term. He was duly adopted by his biological father and did not know he had been adopted until he was mature, married, and a father himself. I suspect that the lady who called you on the phone was Therese's son's wife, technically her daughter-in-law. That is, with an outside chance that it was the granddaughter."

Applegate slumped on the banquette, and his aroma got stronger. I had unconsciously been inching away from him all during our conversation so that we were separated by about two feet of upholstery. I stood up and slowly walked around the small table and sat in the chair facing the man. The air was a little sweeter there.

His voice had faded so badly that I had to strain to hear anything he said after that. Herman Applegate was surely the saddest specimen of loser I had encountered in all my years of dealing with bad guys of every type. And Herman wasn't really a bad guy. He was just a nothing in a terrible suit. His last best chance had evaporated, and he had no place to go and nothing to do.

"Mister Riordan, you've been good to me. I appreciate that. When everybody else thought I had killed Therese, you were the one who wasn't sure. Thank you." He produced a dirty handkerchief and mopped his greasy face. "Now I got to suck it up and do something, but I haven't got a notion of what."

I thought about the last of the money in my unexpected bonanza from the bank. "How much would it cost for you to get back to Miami? You should really turn yourself in to the police. I can almost guarantee they'll let you off. If I put up your air fare, you could pay me back after you get going again. How's that sound?"

He raised his head and managed a wan smile. "You'd do that for me? After I've caused you so much trouble?"

"You haven't caused me any trouble, Herman. Armand Colbert caused me all the trouble when he sent me to Miami. You just happened to be a part of his Aunt Therese's life. You were in the wrong place at the wrong time. Maybe if you get back to Miami and hook up again with the Soul of Discretion Escort Service, you'll be able to get your life going. Okay?"

I told Applegate to drop by my office and I'd write him a check. Although I felt a sharp pang about the money, and was absolutely certain I'd never get it back, it was the thing to do. Herman had nobody to give a damn for him and I didn't really give a damn, either, but, hell, you can't turn a hungry dog away from your door, and I couldn't abandon Herman. Funny thing, though, four weeks after I gave him the air fare and put him on the plane for Florida, he sent me the money. No interest, mind you, but the full principal. What's that thing about casting your bread on the water? That's supposed to get you a profit, isn't it? Even just getting the money back was a revelation, though.

Balestreri was not very understanding about my generosity to Herman. "You are one dumb sonofabitch, Riordan," he said, when I told him about it. "You still don't know whether the bastard is innocent or guilty. As far as I'm concerned, he's still a suspect. Not so much as he was originally, but, shit, he *could* be the bad guy."

"Forget it, Tony. Your murderer is either a tall, gray haired guy in a dark suit, or a female of some description or other. Herman is out of it."

"What makes you so sure? You've been running your ass off without pay on this thing for weeks. And you've got no more now than when you started. Now you've paid this clod's way back to Miami out of your own pocket. If I didn't know about your service record and your numerous arrests for punching people out in saloons, I'd think you were a real wimp."

"Be that as it may, Sergeant. Right now I feel too goddam tired to care what you think. And there's a suspicion down deep in my gut that bothers me a very great deal. You read mystery books, Tony? You know, where the most likely suspect is never the real criminal. And the one who seems the most innocent turns out to be the killer. A lot of 'em wind up like that. The butler done it, you know. Or the housemaid. Or the little old lady with the purple shawl. People like that."

Balestreri huffed and puffed and hung up on me. I had called him from my office an hour or so after I left Applegate at his hotel. Then I called Armand and told him that Applegate was leaving and the hotel bill was being sent to him. For my pains I got several minutes of abuse in three different languages which I will not attempt to reproduce here. I mean, I'm no prude, but I'm not really sure how a translation would sound to the delicate American ear. And they always told me there were no obscene words in French. German, yes, but French is pristine. I don't believe it.

Reiko stuck her head into my office. "What's up, partner? I heard you make a couple of calls and then listen for a long, long time. What could make you listen so patiently?

"You mean you managed to stay off the line for a change? It was Armand, love. He hired me to do a job which you and I did. He wanted to eviscerate Herman Applegate when he thought Herman was the murderer. Herman was stashed for a considerable period of time in a hotel. Now Herman is leaving and Armand is stuck with the hotel bill. Understand?"

She made this little moaning sound that she makes so often. "God, I almost forgot about him. Herman, that is. How's he going to get back to Florida?"

"I'm lending him the money," I said, sort of behind my hand.

"What? *You* are lending him the money? You're crazy,

Riordan. Out of your mind. Company money? You can't do that!"

"It's my money. I still have a little in the bank. The guy needs a break." I said it softly, you know, so it would turneth away wrath.

She stared at me for a full minute. "Well. You're supposed to be a tough guy. But you've done something I probably would have done myself. Guess I can't bitch at you for that." Reiko smiled, turned and slid into her desk chair. She was humming when she booted up her computer. Sounded a little like "We Shall Overcome."

# 34
## *"It's just a cockeyed dream."*

DID YOU EVER have a recurring dream? I mean one that keeps coming back, oh, about once a month or so? Not a nightmare, necessarily. Doesn't have to be especially scary, just frustrating and annoying. I've had one for years, and I'm damned if I can think of any reason for it. Psychiatrists seem to think that dreams are an unconscious manifestation of conscious desires or fears. Like the teen-age boy who has had no sexual experiences having what is politely called "nocturnal emissions." Wet dreams, right?

Well, I'm past that stage of life, thank you, by several active decades, so I don't have wet dreams anymore. My oldest repeating dream involves losing my car. Yeah, that's it, losing (or misplacing) my mistreated Mercedes. Goes like this: I park to go to my office, and when I come out I can't find the car. I remember precisely where I parked it, but it isn't there. Or maybe I park in a big lot at a shopping center and mark very carefully the location. Then when I come out, the car is not where I left it. I make endless trips around the block if I'm in town, or exhausting journeys up and down the aisles if I'm in a parking lot. But I never find the car. I wake up. Never do I assume that the car has been stolen. It is simply inconceivable that anybody would steal a fifteen-year-old Mercedes two-seater in such lousy shape.

It's strange but I always remember this particular dream. Lots of times I'm conscious of having dreamt during the night, but I can't recall any details. But I always remember the lost car dream for some mysterious reason.

I'm going through all this because I've been having a different recurring dream for the past week, seems like nearly every night. It has something to do with Therese Colbert's murder, but I'm not exactly sure what. An idea is buried somewhere deep in my subconscious and it's trying to come out.

The dream goes like this: I'm in a courtroom. It's a murder trial. I seem to be the defense attorney. The defendant is seated beside me at a table, but I can't see who he, she or it is. There's the accused, a foot away, and I can't recognize the face or even the gender. It's sort of like when they deliberately blur out the faces of crime suspects in one of those "reality" TV shows. We've apparently finished the trial and are waiting for the jury's verdict. The judge comes in and we all stand up. The jury files into the box and there's the business of handing a slip of paper to the bailiff. The judge hands it back and it's delivered to the jury foreman. He reads: "We the jury, in the matter at hand, find the defendant. . . . " I wake up.

Goddamit, I never hear the verdict, never recognize the defendant. I told you I have a law degree, but I've never practiced. Haven't sat at the defense table since the mock trials we used to have in school. I've testified many times, and I've sat for hours listening to testimony in courtrooms. So the whole dream is very detailed, very real. But it's just a damn' dream.

Why? I've been waking from that dream at four o'clock in the morning and lying in bed until dawn trying to make out the defendant's face.

When I told her about it, Reiko didn't hesitate one second. She said: "It's easy, Riordan. You know in your heart—and in your head—who killed Therese Colbert. But something in you doesn't want to believe it. You are subconsciously blocking out recognition. You're doing it to yourself."

"Bullshit. It's just a cockeyed dream. Doesn't mean a thing. And where do you come off being so goddam smart?"

"Face it, partner. You don't need to be a disciple of Dr. Freud to see what's happening. You've really put all the pieces together in your head, but you don't want to believe what you *know* to be true."

Maybe. I ticked off all the possible suspects: Applegate, Sterns, Martha, Sydney. Who else? Maybelle, Victoria, DiSalvo. Oh, hell, maybe it was just a burglary. Burglar got into Therese's house, couldn't find anything, she came in, he got scared and lost control, grabbed a knife and stabbed the old lady. End of case. Simple.

No. There had been no break-in. Hard to tell if anything was taken from the house. Therese might have had a shoebox full of fifty-dollar bills under the bed or something.

No. This may not have been a premeditated murder, but it was surely second degree, committed in a fit of anger or passion.

So my dream continued to bug me. I had to find out who the defendant of my dream was.

"Has that lawyer gone back to Florida yet? Sterns. Therese's lawyer." I don't know why I asked Reiko.

"Why the hell do you ask me? Call Armand."

When he came on the phone he was annoyed, as usual. "He's still here. He is staying at La Playa. The man is a golf nut, Patrick. He may never go back to Miami."

I called the hotel.

"Hello, Riordan. Any news?"

The lawyer sounded a little breathless, as if I might have caught him in a little midday humping.

"I was just wondering, " I said, "if we could get together

again for a cup of coffee or something. There are still a few details I'd like to clear up. You name the time and the place."

Sterns took his time answering. "I don't see why not. Why don't you come here about three. We can meet in the bar."

"I'll be there. I'll wear a white carnation in my buttonhole so you'll know me. But you know me already, don't you, counselor."

I think we hung up simultaneously. I didn't particularly like Sterns. He was a smooth liar whose lies were rationalized in legal precedents. He hadn't told me what he knew in the beginning, and he probably wouldn't tell me the whole story now. But I had this itchy feeling that somehow I could draw out of him the means of identifying the defendant sitting beside me in my own night court.

# 35
## *The lawyer looked tired.*

THE GUY was punctual, I'll have to say that. Sterns appeared at three o'clock precisely in the cocktail lounge of La Playa. I had been sitting in a booth for about five minutes sipping a cup of coffee.

I made a half-hearted move at standing as he arrived. We shook hands and I noticed how long and thin his fingers were as they wrapped around mine and crunched my knuckles. I'm convinced that guys who really bear down on you in a handshake are closet sadists. My big university class ring bit viciously into my middle and pinkie fingers.

"Well, Riordan, what's on your mind? I really thought you were satisfied that I had told you all I know about *everything*. Sorry I had to omit a few things in the beginning. I had sworn to Therese Colbert that I would never breathe a word about our arrangement or Sydney or the phony Schwab Foundation."

"Why 'Schwab,' counselor? Why'd you pick that name?"

"No special reason. It's a brokerage I do business with. Seems to have a sort of neutral, heartland sound. Just a whim, I guess."

I studied the man as he lit a long brown cigarette.

"Oh, I'm sorry," he said. "I should have asked permission. Mind if I smoke?"

I did, but I didn't say it. No point in it. Some guys still hang onto the habit, even though it's a statistical certainty that a lot of 'em will wind up dead too soon.

"Counselor, would you mind going back through the story, starting with Therese's first contact with you about her will."

He sat back against the plastic upholstery of the booth and blew smoke at the ceiling. "I have a lot of elderly lady clients in the northeast quadrant of Miami. And most of 'em are in the same situation. They're alone, they've lived there for a long time, they don't want to move, and they're loaded. Widows, mostly. Husbands who owned small businesses and worked their asses off, retired, and then died in a couple of years from the stress of making all the money. Somebody, one of her friends, referred Therese to me.

"She made an appointment and came into my office to discuss a will. God, I remember how hard it was to get anything out of her. She was reluctant at first to tell me just what assets she had. We didn't accomplish anything in that first meeting. She just left and said she *might* be back.

"She did come back a month or so later. Apparently she'd been doing a lot of thinking, trying to convince herself of what she really wanted to do.

"I'll never forget that second meeting. She sat there and told me the whole story of her life. All of her lovers, her mediocre career in show business, the affair with Hammer, the pregnancy, the son, the granddaughter. What she wanted to do was set up this dummy corporation as her principal heir, with Armand as personal representative and residual beneficiary. The corporation was to be in the name of her son and/or his heirs or assigns as sole owners. Then we'd work

151

out a way for Armand to supervise the probate without knowing about Bruce Hammer or Sydney. It turned out to be sort of a mouse-in-a-maze operation because of all the details Therese insisted on. All those addresses and telephone numbers cost her a goodly chunk of money. She had to pay for the answering service in Sacramento, the rental in Chinatown, lots of little shit that she just had to have."

What kind of woman would go to the trouble of setting up such a bizarre network just to conceal the fact that she had given birth to an illegitmate child fifty-odd years ago? Therese Colbert was a woman of her own time, I guess. She couldn't bring herself to admit her terrible sin to anybody but an attorney who, she thought, would be bound by the well-known lawyer-client relationship not to reveal her deep, dark secret. So she hatched, with the attorney's help, this Byzantine arrangement to enable her to leave most of her assets to her only but unacknowledged child.

"Okay, counselor. I accept all that, even though I'm not sure I understand it. What I'm really interested in is just what you talked with her about during those visits you made to Therese's house just before her death. You say you discussed the will. You say you were trying to talk her out of marrying Applegate and running off with him. Anything else? Surely, if the will was already a matter of record, she must have suggested changing it. Or there wouldn't have been any reason to call you to the house."

Sterns was still dragging on the long brown cigarette that he'd lit a few minutes ago, but he abruptly took it from his lips and stubbed it out in a glass ashtray. He took his time as he stared intently at the remains of the cigarette, grinding it carefully far longer than necessary.

"You might have guessed it, Riordan. What the lady wanted to do was change her will to reduce Sydney's share to a small bequest and settle most of her money on Herman Applegate. She knew that Bruce had died. She knew that Martha and Sydney were alienated. She had never known any of them as adults, but she had felt the obligation to her own flesh and blood in the case of Bruce. Apparently, she didn't have much of a sense of responsiblity towards Sydney, and even less towards Martha."

The lawyer looked tired. I guess he must have felt sort of wrung out. He had done his duty honestly, I guess. But it took a lot out of him. I sensed that despite his predilection for golf, he'd rather be back in Miami.

"Thanks," I said. "You've cleared up a couple of things for me. Maybe you've done more than that. I don't know right now. But you look bushed, counselor. When are you going back to Florida?"

"As soon as possible. You see, there's this woman I met in a bar up on Ocean Avenue that just won't take no for an answer, and. . . . "

"Thanks again, counselor. I sure appreciate your cooperation." I started to leave as he fumbled for another of those long, brown, stinking cigarettes.

"Wait a minute, Riordan," he called. "Have you thought about the story outline I told you about. You know, about the young lawyer and the dishonest law firm?"

"Why yes, counselor. Sounds great. Guy named Grisham already wrote it. He could give you some pointers."

It was cruel and I knew it, but I couldn't resist this time. The man looked absolutely crushed as I left him in the bar.

I drove up Eighth Avenue and made a left on Junipero. Armand was going to have to be told about what I got from his aunt's lawyer. A parking space opened up just below Fifth on the center strip. There are no parking restrictions along the center divider of Junipero, so it's almost always a hundred percent used during the day. I was lucky. As I walked down Fifth towards Armand's place, I glanced into the patio restaurant of the General Store at the corner.

Sitting at one of the small wooden tables were my sometime client, Armand Colbert, and his new-found first cousin, once removed, or something like that, Sydney Hammer.

153

# 36
## *It was a beautiful day in Carmel.*

NEITHER OF THEM looked up as I approached, and I stood by their table for thirty or forty seconds before they realized I was there. They must have thought I was a waiter or a bus boy.

"'Scuse me, folks, would the little lady like another glass of wine?" I asked, in what I thought was a waiterly fashion.

Armand looked up, startled. "Pat. I didn't expect to see you here. Now. Uh, Sydney and I, we were just getting acquainted. It's somewhat of a shock to discover that one has a cousin so near, and yet. . . . "

"So far? Hi, Sydney. I didn't know you were in town . . . again. What'd you do? Quit DiSalvo's law firm? Or are you taking a well-earned vacation? You're pretty rich now. Why don't you buy Armand's restaurant. It does real well, I think. That right, Armand?"

"I'm not going to ask you to sit down, Riordan. Sydney and I have a good deal to discuss. It's a family matter, you understand. There, run along like a good fellow. Call me later if you have anything to say to me."

I sat down anyhow. "I just thought I ought to tell you that your attorney friend from Florida has informed me that it was Therese's desire to change her will, leaving only a token amount to Sydney and the bulk of the estate to Herman. She wanted to dissolve the Schwab Foundation. The noble Sterns was trying to dissuade her from this abrupt change, which is why he visited her house several times in the week before her death. Thought that might be interesting to you. You, too, Sydney. By the way, why Sydney? Was you father just back from Australia when you were born?"

She looked very uncomfortable. "Sydney is my mother's maiden name. She was Martha Sydney. It's a prominent family name in Marin County. Old money, you know."

"Old money? Dear, your sweet mama told me that your father's death left her practically destitute. What happened to that 'old money'?"

"My grandfather died broke. No, worse than that. He died owing nearly four hundred thousand dollars. That's my maternal grandfather, you understand. Andrew Sydney. My father's father paid his debts. My father didn't have much in his own right. He was an attorney, but he was working on a novel."

My God, I thought. Are all the lawyers writing novels? Poor Bruce Hammer. Too bad he died young.

I have found, in the practice of my trade, that as often as not if you manage to scrape off the top layer of a puzzlement, the underlayers tend to peel rather easily. Sterns' revelation of the genesis of the Schwab Foundation and the somewhat goofy plans laid by Therese Colbert to make sure that her son was heir to most of her estate opened up a whole new avenue of investigation. I began to feel like one of those dogged, perceptive inspectors in an Agatha Christie mystery. I do not have the brilliant insight of Hercule Poirot, but I can recognize an obvious clue when one falls into my lap.

155

It must have been just about at this point, during my conversation with Armand and Sydney in the General Store's patio that the clouds began to drift away on a gentle ocean breeze. I apologized for interrupting a family discussion and quietly slipped away. Out of the corner of my eye as I left the patio, I saw Armand reach across the table and gently take Sydney's hand. I don't really know if it's true about cousins getting romantically involved, but I knew that Armand was considered the most charming and eligible bachelor on the Peninsula. My late wife, Helen, used to say that he could charm the pants off any woman and probably did. I must have paused to stare because he turned in my direction quickly and shot a nasty glare my way. I hurried out.

It was a beautiful day in Carmel. When the weather is right there's just no place like it. The only problem is that when the weather is right the visitors clog the town. I don't just mean the busloads of tourists disgorged every hour at the Plaza. But on any given weekend during the extended summer season, and often during the week, there are visitors from Southern California as well as the surrounding territory, including Santa Cruz, San Jose, Oakland and San Francisco. People from Salinas, seventeen miles inland come out to the coast to escape the heat. Highway One is bumper-to-bumper in both directions, north and south. South to Point Lobos and Big Sur. North from Hearst Castle and San Luis Obispo. They all fight for position on poor little, two-lane Highway One. Every now and then a few miles south a carload of visitors will be taking in an ocean view and drift over the center line for a spectacular head-on collision.

We can always tell when the fire wagons and ambulances start screaming through town, headed south.

I love the place, though. And now that I'm a homeowner and a taxpayer, I feel even more that I'm part of the town. It's an odd place, though, with a population that is difficult to count because so many people who own houses here just visit occasionally. The last population figure I heard was 4,300.

But I don't think there are that many people occupying homes at any given time.

The hood on the Mercedes was still warm when I went back to the car. My mission had been to talk to Armand alone in his office. But there was little Sydney, looking fresh and pretty and demure, allowing her tiny hand to be held by her fortyish cousin. I sat in the car without opening the windows for a while before I realized I was suffocating.

I drove slowly up Junipero and out of town by the truck route. Lost in thought, I nearly missed the Munras Avenue turnoff and the guy behind me leaned on his horn as I crossed his path at the last second. On Pacific, my thoughts began to form a conclusion that I didn't like very much.

Reiko looked up from her computer and stared at me.

"What's the matter, Reiko-san? Have I grown another head? Is my nose running? Is my fly open? What?"

"You are in one of those semi-trances that you always get in when you're preoccupied. Do you remember where you parked?"

"Hell, yes, I remember where I parked," I said, vehemently, although at that moment I *couldn't* remember. I strode indignantly into my office and sat down in my padded, reclining office chair.

She appeared in the doorway.

"I know you, mister. You're wrestling with something that bothers the hell out of you, aren't you? It's like that dream business, isn't it? I *told* you. You've got it all worked out, but you don't want to believe it. You're . . . what's the popular phrase? 'In denial'. Right?"

"Go away. Go play with your state-of-the-art electronics. Leave me alone for a while."

"Okay. But when you come out of the clouds, try to remember that I called it as I saw it. I'm never wrong."

She left and quietly closed the door.

There's only one person I can depend on for sympathy. Most of the time. I punched out Sally Morse's number.

"What's the matter, Pat? Make it swift. I've got a lot of work to do."

"Sal, you haven't been up to my house yet. How about coming by for a glass of wine and a piece of cheese this evening?"

"I haven't come up to your house because you haven't got enough furniture for me to be able to sit down."

"Oh, but I have. Reiko and her mama have given me the use of some stuff temporarily. I've even got a love seat, if you're in the mood."

"You don't make love on a love seat. It's too damn' short. But if you'll buy some decent wine and get something other than Velveeta, I'll come up. When? About five-thirty okay?"

"Great. I need to talk to you, Sal. I am on the horns of a dilemma. I'll get some nice brie at the Fifth Avenue deli."

"You've got a refrigerator, haven't you? I mean, the kitchen is fully equipped, isn't it? You sound sort of melancholy, Patrick. What's up?"

"I'll unburden myself when you get here. And maybe you'll stay for breakfast. I've got a really big bed."

# 37
## *"She proposed to me, Pat."*

CARLOS VESPER, turban askew, burst into my office with Reiko grimly hanging onto his loose Indian shirt.

"Riordan, you've got to help me," he shouted. "That old woman, that Grimme woman, wants me to marry her."

Reiko gave a yank on the shirt tail that almost threw him to the floor. "I'm sorry. I tried to stop him. The guy is obviously out of his mind. But he got past me before I could do *this*." She chopped the man across the shoulder with her right hand and he fell to his knees in obvious pain.

"Get up, Carlos. I know it hurts, but it'll go away in a week or so. There, you can make it. Sit in the nice chair and take a few deep breaths."

Reiko helped Vesper into the only guest chair in my office, and he sat glassy-eyed, rubbing the injured shoulder.

"He's damn lucky I didn't kill him," said my sometimes violent partner. "I could have, y'know. The right chop in the right place. Behave, man, or I'll get you again."

Vesper had the look of a desperate, wounded man. After the short period I allowed for his recovery, I asked him for an explanation.

"She proposed to me, Pat. She backed me against the wall and proposed to me. No woman ever did that before. Not even the cello player for the San Francisco Symphony. No, *she* kicked my ass out of her apartment just because I said she was bowlegged. Flora Grimme proposed to me. Asked *me* to marry her. I gave her such comfort, she said. The personal trainer who came Mondays, Wednesdays and Fridays left her bruised and sore. But I comforted her on Tuesdays and Thursdays. Good God, what am I going to do?"

"Take her up on it, Carlos. She's wealthy. She thinks she's in love with you. She's probably over seventy and you'll outlive her. Think of all you can do with Flora's money. Marry her, you dumb sonofabitch."

He thought it over. "I don't want to. I'm still young, just forty-one. It'd be too miserable. No, I can't do it, Riordan."

"Think about it again," I said. "You won't have to steal anything from her. It'll all be yours. I won't have to go out there and pretend to discover her strongbox. *You* can discover the strongbox. You'll have like a vision where you see where it is and you'll discover it. That'll make you even more of a hero. And when the lady departs this mortal coil, you'll have all those gems for yourself. You can sell 'em legitimately. Or wear 'em. I understand there's one big stone that'd look great on your turban. How about that?"

"Well, maybe . . ."—he was beginning to have dreams of once again possessing a Lamborghini—". . . maybe it wouldn't be so bad." Then another moment of panic. "But I *can't*, Riordan. I'll have to take off my clothes in front of her. She'll see the parts I couldn't expose in the tanning parlor. She'll see the white skin along my hairline that I can cover with the turban. She'll find out I'm a phony."

"That'll happen sooner or later anyhow, Carlos. You are a phony. You've always been a phony. You can't change the spots on a leopard. And Flora can't change you into an honest man. But I have a notion that she'll ignore your shortcomings, even when you drop your pants." I was tempted to laugh out loud, but brought my iron will into play.

Carlos didn't seem to notice my small joke. He was beginning to look his old self. The furrows disappeared from his brow and he smiled a saintly smile.

"You're right. It's the thing to do. She couldn't live forever. But I won't do anything rash, Riordan. I wouldn't think of hastening her demise."

"You better damn' well not, man," I said vehemently. "Don't ever forget I'm here and I know all about you. And if you marry Flora and anything the least little bit suspicious happens to her, I'll know you had a hand in it. You understand me, don't you?"

"Sure. Can't put anything over on you. You had me pegged before. You lent me a hundred bucks. Now I can pay you back. Thanks. I'll invite you and your nasty little partner to the wedding."

That was the last I saw of Carlos Vesper. He didn't invite Reiko and me to the wedding. I did see a note in The Herald about the betrothal of Mrs. Flora Grimme to Maharishi Mehta about two weeks after Carlos had left my office. Maharishi! The man is a goddam genius, all right.

# 38
## "Cherchez la femme, *you know.*"

MURDER, MURDERERS, Red Chinese troops never scared the hell out of me like the process of buying a house. It is possibly the most gut-wrenching experience imaginable aside from giving birth, a phenomenon I, of course, have not experienced.

There are some things you have to watch out for when you buy a house in Carmel, California. The town is all hills, separated by deep ravines which are good ol' Ma Nature's arrangements for drainage in the rainy season. Possibly the best advice I've ever had came from a retired attorney acquaintance, who said: "Never buy a house in a hole."

I didn't know what he meant when he said it. But I've seen a few really wet winters since I heard his pronouncement and it's pretty clear now. A lot of houses are built dead bang at the bottoms of gulllies, mainly because it was the only land available when they were constructed. When the rain pours down in buckets during the heavier rainy seasons the water races

162

down the hills into these little pockets and stays there. You've got to have a device called a sump pump that comes on automatically and pushes the water up out of your yard before it gets in the house.

I didn't realize it at the time, but even though the house I bought was on a hillside, it was better than being in the bottom of what amounts to a box canyon. Whoever built my house must have poured several tons of concrete for the foundation, and even after having gone through the earthquake of '89, it sits firmly in place. Dumb luck on my part, I guess.

Sally arrived just a bit after five o'clock. She must have been burning with curiosity to see what kind of pad I bought. They don't say "pad" anymore, do they? I'm always a step or two behind the latest language, a little late catching the newest phrase. It's like I always swung late at the baseball and popped to right or hit a slow roller down the first base line. I still don't know what "pushing the envelope" means.

"Hmmm," said Sally Morse when she came through my front door. Silently she walked through the kitchen into the dining area which contained no table or chairs. I was still eating breakfast standing over the sink at the time. There's furniture there now, if you want to come up some time.

Sally continued her inspection, walking slowly into the living room, down the hall past the barren second bedroom and guest bath, into the master bedroom. She stopped and stared at the bed. Then, at last, she looked at me.

"Riordan, you have done a good thing. It's a snug little house. And there's more room for my clothes in your closet. How's it heated?

My God, I couldn't tell her. In the whirlwind of paper and the enervating process of buying the house, I hadn't even asked about a furnace. "I—I don't know, honey. It hasn't been all that cold, and I haven't spent a lot of time here."

"There are heat outlets in the floor, Riordan. There's one and there's one. There is a thermostat in the living room. You *must* have a furnace. Where is it?"

163

"I guess it's down under. Where else would it be? Are you cold, Sal? Want a blanket or something?"

"Let's go back into the living room. We can sit down on that love seat and talk. I suspect that you're not entirely in your right mind. It's the thing about that old woman in Florida, isn't it? Armand's aunt."

We sat down and Sally held my hand as I brought her up to date on the frustrating case of the wealthy chorus girl who wound up dead in Miami Shores. She listened patiently as I told her of the twists and turns of the dead lady's love life and her obsession with secrecy. The creation of the Schwab Foundation seemed to interest her most.

"Why in God's name would the woman insist on creating a dummy corporation just so she could leave her money to her illegitimate son? What kind of nutty old broad was she, anyhow?"

"I have frequently asked myself the same question, Sal. But I'm afraid people who live by themselves for long periods of time get to be a little eccentric. Make that 'nutty', if you like. Doesn't that suggest anything to you?"

"You're saying that I'll go bananas from living by myself. You're proposing to me again, Riordan. That's it, isn't it?"

Same old story. I have proposed to Sally a dozen or more times in a dozen or more ways, and she has always turned me down.

I mustered up my courage. "Well, how about it? You weren't crazy about George's house at Sixth and Santa Rita. Okay, now I have my own place down here on Santa Fe. Any time, Sal, any time."

She squeezed my hand and looked at me for a long time. Then she leaned toward me and kissed me. Abruptly, she got up.

"I've got to go. You'll appreciate the fact that I didn't say 'no'. Didn't say 'yes', either. But, Patrick . . . I'm beginning to warm up to the idea. Call me tomorrow morning and we'll have lunch."

"Hey, you haven't even had any cheese, goddamit. And I got an expensive bottle of wine just for you. I can't drink the stuff and you know it." I didn't know whether to be happy or angry. She would and she wouldn't. She did and she didn't. But for some reason, I began to feel a warm glow.

"You haven't drawn the cork, have you? So save the wine. I have a hunch it'll come in handy."

"All right. I'll call you about ten. But I'm still stuck with this goddam murder case, and I don't know where to go with it."

"You don't? I thought you were smarter than that. From what you told me, it's pretty clear. You'd better check out your innocent little Sydney a bit more carefully, Patrick. *Cherchez la femme*, you know. Do you know where she was the week before you flew off to Florida? Where you and Reiko stayed all night in *one* hotel room."

How in hell did she find that out? Sally has ways. Kinda makes me feel good, really. She *cares*. She keeps track of me. She loves me, by God.

I walked her to her car and saw her on her way. As I waved goodbye, it dawned on me that she might have cut away all the muck that obscured Therese's murder and come up with was to her something obvious that I had missed. "You'd better check out your innocent little Sydney," she said.

Yeah, I'd better.

# 39
## *"You're really whipped, you know that?"*

Reiko STARED incredulously at me. "Sydney? You got to be kidding, round eyes. And you want *me* to question her about her whereabouts the week before we went to Miami. Now, listen up. Sydney Hammer is no more capable of murder than I am. I *know* these things. It's women's . . . "

"Stop! Don't give me the old 'intuition' bit. Women are no more intuitive than pandas. Well, maybe pandas. But nowhere is it written that women have powers that defy explanation. Especially when it comes to other women."

My small sansei partner is not often nonplussed, but at that moment she looked at least confused. "Sally's never met Sydney, Riordan. How could she suspect. . . . "

"I don't know. I told her the whole story in detail. That's before I proposed to her again. And she just said I'd better find out where Sydney was at the time of Therese's death. I didn't ask her to explain."

"You asked her to marry you again? Aren't you getting

damn sick and tired of doing that? You're a glutton for punishment. You're really whipped, you know that? And what did she say? Maybe? Like she always says."

"Never mind. Will you talk to Sydney or not? Do I have to do clumsily what you do so well? I mean, if I come right out and ask her, she'll know she's suddenly become a suspect. But if you can draw her out, with all your smooth oriental subtlety, she won't think it's anything out of the ordinary."

"You're on one of your 'least suspicious character' kicks, aren't you. Well, smartass, I'll talk to the lady. And, believe me, there's not a doubt in my mind that she's innocent as a new-born babe."

She marched out into her office and slammed the door.

Maybe I should have gone on and practiced law, as Sterns had suggested. Sterns is thinking of writing a book. But the guy from Mississippi beat him to it. That guy's been making all kinds of money writing books. If I had really practiced courtroom law, I could write a book that would sell a million copies. But my fiance dumped me just before my bar exam and I went out and got disgustingly drunk. To say that I flunked the exam would be an understatement. I had trouble *seeing* the exam.

But if I had passed . . . goddamit I'd be in pig heaven now. Like Sterns. And the Mississippi guy. Collecting big fees for my services. Writing books. Touring the country in style. Being recognized in restaurants. Being dogged by photographers from the *Globe* and the *National Enquirer.* I practiced a faint smile and a friendly wave.

My office door opened and Reiko stuck her head in. "I've invited Sydney down for the weekend. Just to be sociable. Just to be a friend. She'll be here Friday night. You're going to regret asking me to do this, Riordan. I'm taking her out to dinner at Fresh Cream Friday and down to the Highlands Inn Saturday. It's all going on the expense account."

She pulled her head back and slammed the door again.

Ah, Reiko. What would I do without her? She can be an

unbearable pain in the ass sometimes. But she's so smart and so loyal. I had never really known an Asian person before I met Reiko. Yeah, I fought North Koreans and Chinese way back in those forgotten, pre-Eisenhower days. And I had spent some leave time in Japan. But I was very young, and I was still trying to figure out why on the one hand we were trying to kill North Koreans who looked just South Koreans who were our allies, and taking R&R in Japan where the people looked just about the same to a naive GI, although *they* had been the enemy not even a decade before. I think it was about that time that I thought of trying to find one of those Indian gurus who could tell me the Meaning of Life.

The telephone woke me from my little session of remembrances of things past.

"Riordan, it's Sterns. I called to say good-bye. I'm catching a commuter to San Francisco and will be back in Miami tonight. Good luck on running down Therese's killer. You've got my office number if you need anything from me."

I had hardly hung up the phone when it rang again.

"Hello, Mr. Riordan. This is Herman Applegate. Just thought I'd let you know that I'm leavin'. I'll turn myself in to the cops when I get back to Miami. Will you call 'em or write 'em and tell 'em I didn't ever run away. While I was here, that is. Will you tell 'em, please."

I had sort of an uneasy feeling. Two of my suspects were soon going to be more than three thousand miles away. But, hell, it wasn't my responsiblity to catch the murderer of Therese Colbert. The Miami cops and the Metro-Dade force were directly involved. I was a simple-minded private investigator in California whose interest was, well, *personal*. I found the old lady's body. I was not going to rest until I found out for sure who killed her.

A couple of days passed without incident. No, that's not true. There were a couple of incidents. Some tourist looking for a place to park stopped suddenly in front of me and I tapped his bumper. And an over-zealous waiter in the restaurant where Sally and I were having lunch took my plate away before I had a chance to mop up my spaghetti sauce with my French bread. That was some luncheon. Sally was as non-committal as she ever was.

"What did you mean when you said 'I'm beginning to warm up to the idea'?" I was determined to pursue what I perceived to be an advantage.

"Not much," she said. "Patrick, I love you. And I enjoy being with you. But I'm still not sure that I'd enjoy being with you all the time."

"You wouldn't be with me all the time. You have your work and I have mine. We'd just have evenings and weekends. And nights, of course." I didn't want to seem like a sex fiend.

"I know. You had a happy marriage. You and Helen must have been perfectly matched. And you were devastated when she was killed. But I had a bad marriage. My husband was a trumpet player. He was almost never at home. He was on the road or jamming all night. We're friends now, but we had a pretty nasty divorce. See the difference?"

"Yeah, I see the difference. But Jimmy Morse was Jimmy Morse, and I'm *me*. It just ain't the same thing."

Sally leaned back and closed her eyes. "Maybe you're right. Tell you what. What's today? Thursday? Okay, you come out to my place Sunday and I'll give you an answer. I don't want to see you before Sunday, understand?"

I had to accept her terms. And I had some thinking to do myself. I had to decide if I was eager for marriage because I was madly in love with Sally or if I was just sick of living alone and seeing my relationship with my first and so far only wife through a glass dimly tinted rose. Well, I'd find out Sunday.

# 40
## *"Keep a stiff upper lip and a tight sphincter."*

SATURDAY MORNING I was awakened out of a very deep sleep by the irritating sound of the telephone. I glanced at my bedside digital clock and determined that it was quarter after nine. I had been dreaming the long and involved dream about finding my car in a giant parking lot, and the phone had rung just as I was about to find the car or be hit by a speeding pickup, I couldn't remember which.

"Riordan, it's me," said Reiko, much too loudly for the early hour. "You're still in bed, aren't you. Well, Sydney's here and I think you ought to talk to her."

"Is she *there?* I mean, with you?"

"Nope. She insisted on taking a room at that bed and breakfast place down on Central. She'd never been in one of those, she said. Wanted to find out what it was like. I said I'd pick her up at ten. You want us to come over to your house? Or go to the office?"

For the first half hour after awakening, I am inclined to be slow in making decisions. I pulled my thoughts together with some effort, fully aware that Reiko was impatiently waiting at the other end of the line.

"Ummm," I said, "not here. This place isn't ready for out-of-town visitors yet. And I hate like hell to have to make the bed on a Saturday morning. Let's meet at the office at, uh, ten-thirty."

Reiko's voice was softer now. "Okay. I . . . sort of . . . broached the subject of her whereabouts during the time in question, y'know. She told me, Pat, she had it all down to the hour. But . . . I dunno. Maybe it was too precise, too calculated. Well . . . you can judge for yourself when you talk to her. I had a hell of a time finding a way to ask her the big question. Just asked her if she'd had a vacation recently. Yeah, she said, she and a girl friend had gone to Disney World in Orlando. At just the time we were talking about. I still don't think she could have killed the woman who was her grandmother. But. . . . "

"See you in about an hour, babe. Keep a stiff upper lip and a tight sphincter. I'll be very delicate. Right now I have to think of some questions to ask the young lady."

Getting out of bed at my age is not the easiest thing in the world. It is best done slowly. First you sit up, then you swing your legs over one at a time. Pause for thirty seconds to let the circulation reach the brain. Groan about the aches and pains that come from various moving parts. Stand. Move to the bathroom and pee. Wash face and comb hair. Shave.

Like most men, I spend very little time selecting a wardrobe for the day. As often as not, it's the wardrobe from yesterday. After all, primitive man went forth with just an animal skin or two and a lot of body hair. What the hell.

Sydney and Reiko were in the office chattering like a couple of high school cheerleaders on a crowded rooters' bus. When I entered, they both turned cheerful faces towards me.

"Hello, ladies. Nice to see you again, Sydney. Can I buy you both a cup of coffee and a Danish? Or accompany you for a stroll on Fisherman's Wharf? Or something?" I had not yet figured out how to approach Sydney's vacation.

"Thank you, no. I saw the Wharf on the last trip. It's okay if you like seafood restaurants, but I wouldn't want to spend much time there." Sydney looked radiant. She was the picture of beautiful innocence. Well, she was *rich*.

I took a chance. "Reiko tells me you were at Disney World recently. Just what kind of place is it? I've been to Disneyland a couple of times. But the other place—is it different? Better? Bigger?"

She smiled broadly. "It's about the same. Lots of things to do, things to see. I was there with Denise from our office. She's a Florida girl, born in Ocala. She hadn't seen her parents for some years."

"Oh, then you went over to Ocala. How'd you like Silver Springs? You know, the glass-bottom boat thing."

"Sorry, I didn't go to Silver Springs. Denise went alone. It was sort of a family reunion."

"Then you stayed at Disney World. For a day or so by yourself?"

She smiled disarmingly again. "Well, not exactly by myself. I met this man—from New Jersey somewhere—and we got to be good friends. Denise was gone for, oh, three days, I think. But I wasn't lonely."

Three days. In Florida. Not really accounted for. Some guy from New Jersey. Couldn't ask his name. Wouldn't do any good. New Jersey is a thickly populated state. How could I push it further? No good to talk to Denise, whoever she was. She had folks in Ocala, maybe sixty miles from Orlando by freeway.

"Did you rent a car, Sydney? How did Denise get to Ocala?"

Her smile was fading a bit. "We did rent a car and Denise drove it up to Ocala." The smile disappeared. "Why all the questions? What is it about my vacation trip that is so interesting to you?"

Reiko had gone to the window in my office and was staring out at Alvarado Street.

"When was the last time you talked with your mother, Sydney? Was it before you flew off to Disney World?"

Her eyes widened. She looked at me in disbelief, then jerked her head around to look at Reiko, who studiously refused to return her gaze.

"What are you getting at, Riordan? What has my mother got to do with all this? Why are you asking me all these stupid questions?"

I didn't answer. "Was it a spur of the moment decision, going to Florida? Was it Denise's idea . . . or yours? I can ask Denise, you know. If there is a Denise working in your office."

Sydney stood up and turned fiercely on Reiko. "You! You invited me down her so this clown could ask me a lot of dumb questions. You made it sound like a friendly invitation. But it was kind of a trap, wasn't it, Reiko. Your smartass partner here got you to drag me down here so he could try to intimidate me. Well, I'm out of here."

And she was.

# 41
## *"You still think she's a babe in arms."*

"THE LADY doth protest too much." Thanks to good ol' Will of Stratford-upon-Avon for the proper phrase. Sydney Hammer had reacted badly. She had obviously been shaken. I couldn't say for sure why. Was it anger at Reiko for inviting her to Monterey under false pretenses? Or was there some sort of guilt reaction? No way I could know . . . then.

When Sydney had left the office, Reiko and I just sat and stared at each other for a full five minutes. I don't think I had ever seen Reiko looking so terribly depressed. She's usually such an upbeat person, so unflappable and feisty. But during my soft-pedaled questioning of Sydney Reiko had stared out my window through the fly-specks and the bird shit. Now she looked as if her dog had just been run over, except that she didn't have a dog.

"Why did you make me do that?" she asked.

"I didn't *make* you do that, dear. You just accepted a challenge. You were dead certain that Sydney was an innocent lamb, and you were going to prove it to me. Neither of us thought that the episode would end with the lady stomping out of here in a serious snit."

"*Snit!* How can you dismiss that girl's reaction as a *snit*. She was wounded, Riordan. And I'm to blame."

"Hey, wait a minute. You still think she's being persecuted by me. You still think she's a babe in arms."

"I'm not sure what I think. But you've got to admit that nothing she said in this office could come anywhere close to being evidence of guilt. You're guilty of malicious extrapolation, Riordan."

"And you, my dear little friend, are ignoring the obvious," I said. Then I stopped cold. This was the first time that Reiko and I had got into a really serious argument. We have badgered each other a lot, and we've bickered over trifles, but up to that day in my office after Sydney Hammer had fled, we had never had such a grim argument.

"I'm going for a walk," said Reiko. She left the room and I could hear her footsteps as she went down the steep, dark stairs. I went to the window and watched her emerge into Alvarado Street and walk towards the bay into a stiff breeze that mussed her glossy black hair. I wondered when—if—she'd come back. Oh, hell, I thought, she'll come back. She just needs to be alone with her thoughts. I've got to admit that she's seldom been wrong about anything. And as I watched her disappear from my field of vision, I wasn't sure she was wrong this time.

But I had to pursue my own suspicions, and there were certain things I couldn't put off. I reached for the phone.

In a couple of minutes, I had Giuseppe DiSalvo's office on the phone. The lawyer had me put on hold for what seemed to be a quarter of an hour before he deigned to accept my call.

"Yes, Riordan, what is it?" He sounded annoyed.

"Sydney Hammer was on vacation in Florida a week or so before I went there and found Therese Colberts's body. Do you have a woman named Denise something in your office?"

"Sydney did take a vacation. And we do have Denise Carpenter. She and Sydney are very close. I'm not especially fond of Denise because I cannot stand that southern drawl of hers, but she does her work well. Is that what you wanted to know?"

"Thanks. Sorry to trouble you." I hung up.

Damn! Just when I thought I had unraveled some of the strange cloak of mystery surrounding the death of Therese Colbert, there has to be a real, live Denise. I didn't even think at the time that a Carpenter and a Hammer naturally go together. That is a very bad joke. I wish I hadn't thought of it.

Miss Masuda, my favorite partner, poked her head in my door about then and said: "I'm sorry. I didn't mean to walk out on you like that. You were just doing what you thought you had to do. You're a sonofabitch sometimes, but I still love you a little." The head disappeared and in seconds I could hear the tell-tale start-up noises of her computer. I have no idea why she goes to that machine in moments of stress. Somehow, the glow of the screen and the many functions she calls upon give her solace and strength. She has a modem and can summon any number of cheerful facts about the square of the hypotenuse from one of the many far-flung sources she taps. A lady of infinite grace and wisdom is Reiko. And she loves me a little. Not as much as she loves Greg Farrell, I guess. But then I come from a whole different generation.

After a bit I heard her talking to somebody. Probably Farrell, I thought. But moments later I found out I was wrong. She entered the room leading—Sydney Hammer.

## 42
# *A strange development, indeed.*

HER FACE WAS tear-stained, although I couldn't tell right away whether it was from emotion or the stiff breeze that was whistling up Alvarado Street from the bay. She looked somehow smaller than she had looked before, as though she had shrunk from the time she had left my office until she stood before my desk again. I rose from my chair..

"Hello, Sydney. I didn't expect you back so soon." It was a pretty lame greeting, but I didn't know what else to say. "Sit down. The chair ain't comfortable, but it's all I've got."

She sat, with Reiko standing close behind her with her hand on Sydney's shoulder. She spoke slowly and hesitantly.

"It was pretty plain. Reiko had told you that I had been to Florida. You were trying to find out from me if I had gone to Miami. When I told you about Denise visiting her family in Ocala it was the absolute truth. But when I said I had met the guy from New Jersey, I was lying. When Denise left me, I took the first flight I could get from Orlando to Miami. I went to see my . . . grandmother. And the trip to Disney World gave me the opportunity to meet Therese Colbert. I knew that Denise was planning the family reunion thing, and I knew I'd have time to get down to Miami and back while she was gone.

"It was one of the biggest disappointments of my life, Mr. Riordan. When I found my grandmother's house, I was appalled by the look of the neighborhood. And when she answered the doorbell, she opened the door only as far as the chain would allow and stared at me. She asked me what I wanted. She didn't give money to people at the door, she said. She didn't want whatever I was selling. All I could see, really, was her eyes, and they were cold and mean.

"I said, 'I'm your granddaughter. Your son's only child. I'm Sydney Hammer.' Her eyes never changed. She closed the door and I heard her detach the chain. When she opened the door to let me in, she had not lost the forbidding expression."

Sydney closed her eyes, as if she could see the old woman who was her grandmother. She had her hands clasped in her lap. Reiko had both of *her* hands on Sydney's shoulders and was squeezing them hard.

"She looked *evil*, Mr. Riordan. Oh, maybe I just expected her to look evil, I don't know. She had on a sort of caftan and her hair was in curlers. She led me into her living room and pointed to a chair. I sat down. Then she said, 'Young woman, you may well be who you say you are. That is no matter to me. I'm changing my will. My son is dead. I feel nothing for you. I do not know you. I did not really know my son, but I gave birth to him. There is nothing you can do to change my mind. Now, please, I'd like you to leave. I have a dinner engagement.' That's what she said. I can't forget it. It's word for word."

"Did you leave?" I asked. I guess I was waiting for some confession of guilt.

"I left. I went out of that house, got into the car I had rented for the day, and drove to the airport. I was in Miami for about three and a half hours, no more. I did not kill my

178

grandmother. I didn't like her. She was hateful to me. But I couldn't have killed her. Not in a million years."

"At that time, Sydney, did you know about Therese's will. I mean, you were working in DiSalvo's office in San Francsco. You picked up the stuff from that mailbox in that dirty hall on Grant Avenue. Surely, you must have known something about the will."

"I did not know about a will, Mr. Riordan, believe me. As a matter of fact, my mother had only told me about my grandmother a couple of months before I went to Florida. Up to that time I had thought of Edwin Hammer's wife as my grandmother, despite the story about the romance with the showgirl . . . who turned out to be Therese Colbert."

"How did you happen to go to work for DiSalvo? It seems to be such a strange coincidence. That you would be in DiSalvo's office without knowing about the connection with the fictitious Schwab Foundation."

"My mother got me the job. She and DiSalvo had been friends for a long time. As a matter of fact, DiSalvo is my mother's lawyer."

Oops, whole new train of thought. Martha and Giuseppe. Now there's a lovely tie-in. A strange development, indeed. I looked hard at Sydney. It is my conceit that I can read people. Sydney sat before me, windblown and tearful. Maybe she didn't stab her grandma with a kitchen knife. Maybe she was an innocent as she looked. Maybe Reiko was right . . . again.

Reiko knelt beside the chair and put an arm around Sydney. "Okay, honey, let me take you back to your bed and breakfast so you can clean up a little. I'm still taking you to the Highlands Inn tonight for dinner. You'll like that. Say goodbye to Riordan. He's a bully and a boor sometimes, but he means well."

I watched the two of them leave, Reik so small and compact, Sydney so willowy and blonde. I put my feet up on my desk and sighed. I was kind of glad Reiko was right. Or I thought she was right. I still had reservations. And they were certainly not at a hotel in Miami.

# 43
## *He didn't show much reaction.*

I NEEDED SOME fresh air. It's not that I'm a health nut, you understand. Jogging and stair-stepping and all that jazz do not appeal to me at all. I do not own an exercise tape, although I do like to look at some of the ladies who demonstrate on 'em. No, I needed fresh air to clear my head.

Clapping on a tattered wool hat from Ireland that I wear against the often chilly breezes of the Monterey Peninsula, I carefully locked the office door and descended into Alvarado Street.

Not many tourists out today, I thought. Not the season yet. Just a few locals shopping, although the empty store fronts that have appeared in recent months make me uneasy. Alvarado Street used to run all the way to old Fisherman's Wharf until they chopped some of it off for a hotel and convention center. It had more character then, to my way of thinking.

I leaned into what was by now a stiff wind from the bay, and walked down to Del Monte. Turned left for a block to

Calle Principal and, for some dumb reason, went into the lobby of the Mariott. My feet were bothering me, so I sat down on a couch near the bank of elevators.

It's not clear in my mind how long I was there. I hate to have to fish out my little half glasses to look at my watch and I can't see the damn thing unless I do. But the hairs on the back of my neck all stood to attention when one of the elevator doors opened and out came Martha Hammer, closely followed by Elliott Sterns.

"Hello," I said, cheerfully. "Nice to see you both again. Thought you were on your way back to Miami, Elliott. And you, Mrs. Hammer, I'm hurt that you didn't call me when you arrived in Monterey. Now, what could you two be so friendly about? Sure beats me."

To say that the pair was shocked would be an understatement. Sterns turned pale and Martha's face contorted with fury.

"Why we are here is none of your business, Riordan. So I don't feel obliged to tell you anything," said Sydney's mother. "Go to hell." This last sentence she pronounced with great emphasis, spacing the words for maximum impact.

She grasped the shaken lawyer's arm and jerked him across the hotel lobby and out the door.

All my suspicions and instincts came together and I was certain that this was the tide in my life that I should take at the flood, following old Stratford Will's advice. But it wouldn't do any good to tail the people out into the street.

Sydney was off somewhere with Reiko. Sydney's mama and the Florida lawyer were in town, even though he had phoned me just to say goodbye. At that time I wasn't sure that young Sydney hadn't been just putting on an act for my benefit. Or if she knew Martha was in town.

I was still sitting on the couch with that scratchy wool Irish hat pulled down to my eyebrows, looking, I am sure, like an unfortunate and unemployed bank president who had just dropped in to take shelter from the wind. A guy I recognized as one of the hotel security people had been looking at me suspiciously. He approached slowly and I looked up.

"Pat Riordan! What the hell are you doing here? Did they evict you? Are you lookin' for a job? I didn't recognize you with that crummy hat on."

"Sorry. Just dropped in to catch my breath. Caught something else instead. I'll be moving along. And don't insult the hat. My late wife bought it for me a long time ago on a junket to Ireland. It keeps the large bare spot on my head warm. *Adios.*"

I walked up Calle Principal to the little walkway that leads over to Alvarado and back to the office. As I unlocked the door, I could hear the telephone ringing. With the door open, I lunged at the phone on Reiko's desk and said, "Riordan and. . . . "

"It's Sterns. I've got to see you. About our encounter in the hotel."

"Where's Martha, Elliott? You must have dumped her pretty quick. What is it? A little romance? Or just one of those casual physical relationships?"

"It's neither. But it's serious. Martha has taken a cab to the airport. I can be in your office in five minutes."

Well, it was actually eight minutes, but the lawyer was true to his word. He had regained some of his color when he came through my door. His lawyerly poise had returned, but he was obviously disturbed. I didn't rise from my chair when he came in and he sat across my desk without being asked.

"What's your analysis of this situation, Riordan? I can probably refute any conclusion you might have reached."

I leaned back and tried to look relaxed, although my heart was beating a little faster and I could feel my blood pressure rise.

"A lady I know told me to *cherchez la femme*, Elliott. I think she was guessing. But now it seems pretty clear to me that it's a female I've been lookin' for. I mean it was a woman who killed Therese Colbert. How's that for an educated guess?"

He didn't show much reaction. "I'll be honest with you, Riordan." I thought that'd be a nice switch. "Martha visited me when she came to Miami. It was apparently a few days after Sydney had visited her grandmother and had told Martha about the old lady's attitude. Martha told me that she was going to try to convince Therese not to change her will. I said I was in total agreement, that Applegate was a bum and an opportunist, and that I had approached Therese with the same argument but had been denied. But Martha was determined, although I told her that it wouldn't do any good."

"Why didn't you tell Armand, counselor? Why didn't you tell me? You knew all along that Martha was in the act, but you didn't say anything. Did she pay you? Were you, in fact, working for her?"

He nodded slowly. "I know it was an unethical thing for an attorney to do. But at the time I saw no harm in doing it. It would come out for everybody's good, I thought."

"Why was Martha here just now? In Monterey? This is the last place I'd expect to see her."

"She came to see me. I wasn't lying when I phoned you that I was leaving. I was on the verge of checking out of the hotel when she arrived. She's a very determined woman, Riordan. I don't think she'd let anything get in her way. I. . . . " He lapsed into silence.

I studied the man. It was quiet in the room. I didn't feel the need to say anything. I think I knew at that moment that this was the end of the line. Sterns stared at the top of my desk.

"Elliott," I said, after a long silence, "I know you didn't kill Therese Colbert. I'm pretty sure Sydney didn't. Applegate is a slob. DiSalvo probably can prove that he hasn't been out of California in years. The two old ladies from Miami Shores are characters out of a sitcom. Who does that leave, counselor? And how are we going to prove it?"

We both stood up and gravely shook hands.

"I've changed my mind about leaving, Riordan. And I can't answer any of your questions. Lawyer-client relationship, you know what I mean. Sorry. You can reach me at the hotel if you . . . find out anything."

## 44
### *"Vicky got a good look at her."*

"MAYBELLE Carothers called," said Reiko the next morning when I arrived in the office.

"What'd she want?"

"I'm not sure. Although she sounded serious and maybe a little excited."

"My God, she and Veronica have spent all their money and they can't get back to Miami. They want to borrow plane fare."

"I don't think so, Riordan. Maybelle hinted that she had some new information. Something that Victoria had forgotten for a while, but all of a sudden remembered."

With a weary sigh, I called the number Maybelle had left.

"Hello," she said. "Who is this?"

"It's Pat Riordan, Maybelle. What can I do for you? I've recommended all the sightseeing tours on the Monterey Peninsula. I'm tapped out of travel information. Why don't you call Sally Morse in Carmel. She's a friend of mine and. . . . "

"Hey, Mister Riordan, Vicky and me, we just got back from Universal Studios, Knotts Berry Farm and Disneyland. Hell, we been all over the place. And we're goin' back down to see Hollywood Boulevard."

"I wouldn't, dear lady. It ain't what it used to be. You'd be disappointed."

"Riordan, I told you we made up our minds to spend some of the money we been savin' up for so long. Neither one of us has any kids. And we ain't gonna be around to appreciate our grand funerals. We got a lot to do before we go back to Florida, if we ever do. Besides, that state'll take all of what's left of our money after the federal government gets through."

"Then what's on your mind?"

"You know, Vicky ain't the brightest person in the world." Her voice grew hushed, as if Victoria were in the room with her.

"Is she there now?" I whispered.

"No. She's down in the souvenir shop pickin' up some more junk. God, that woman loves junk."

"Then why are you talking so softly?"

"She could come in any time now. Anyways, Vicky's memory isn't the greatest, y'know. Just this morning when we woke up, she sat straight up in bed and told me that something had come back to her all of a sudden. There was a woman who visited Therese's house just about a week before the body was discovered. That's what she drew a blank on before."

"A woman? Was it a young woman with blonde hair and a pony tail?"

"No, Vicky is sure it wasn't no blonde chippy type. This was a grown woman. A *big* woman. She come up in a hired car. Had one o' them stickers on the back bumper. Then she knocked on the door and Therese let her in. Vicky didn't see her leave."

"Maybelle, ask Victoria if she could identify the woman if she saw her again."

185

"Oh, there ain't no trouble about that, Mister Riordan. This woman come up to Victoria's front door and knocked. Asked Vicky where Therese lived. Vicky got a good look at her. Wasn't like she saw her from the window."

"Bless you, Maybelle. Now, listen carefully. You and Vicky have to hang around just a little bit longer. I'll need Vicky to eyeball a suspect."

"Oh, we're not fixin' to leave. We like it here. We'll just sit tight until we hear from you. Hey, Mister Riordan, what's this calamari? We been eatin' a lot of it, and we like it, but we've never heard of it. Don't have it in the east at all, I don't think."

"It's a very exotic fish found only in the waters of Monterey Bay, Maybelle. Try abalone, too, if anybody has it."

I didn't have the heart to tell her that calamari is squid. "Calamari" sounds so musical, so Italian. "Squid" is so unappetizing. But it's really good eating. If you're ever in Monterey or Carmel, be sure to try it. But don't call it "squid".

At this point, I was convinced that Martha Hammer had killed Therese Colbert. But proving it was another matter. I put a call in to Lieutenant Alvarez in Miami.

He sounded surprised when he came on the phone. "Riordan, the California private investigator. Why do you call me? Our Mister Applegate has only this morning arrived in Miami. He immediately came to my office and turned himself in. We are proceeding in our case against him. Do you have anything to add."

I remembered what Herman had asked me to do. "Lieutenant, Applegate asked me to tell you that even after he knew he was under suspicion, he didn't try to run away. He just stayed put, waiting for developments until he decided to come back voluntarily. He's innocent, Lieutenant. I'm sure."

"That remains to be seen. I'm not convinced."

"When your lab people examined Therese Colbert's house, did they find any other prints? I know they found Herman's, and I'm sure they found Therese's. Any others."

"Oh, an assortment. Nothing of record. Prints of four or five different people, none of them criminals. At least, none of them in anybody's file."

"Did you try California, Lieutenant? There are some print files out here that you might have overlooked. They take'em for non-criminal reasons. Like, for example, when somebody applies for a teaching credential. There might be others."

"Like when you apply for a private investigator's license? We know you were in the house. Some of the prints were yours. It seems like a futile exercise to me, Mister Riordan. What is on your mind?"

"If I could get a print from somebody for one reason or another, could you run a comparison with the unidentified prints you got at Therese's?"

"Certainly. We have all of them on file, of course. I believe you are wasting your time, man. We have a weapon. We have prints on the weapon. That's enough for me."

"Give me a couple of days, Lieutenant. I may have an eye-witness and a tell-tale print for you."

"These matters move rather slowly in Dade County. You have plenty of time to spin your wheels. Goodbye."

I walked out into Reiko's space and felt her phone. It was warm from her hands and I knew she'd been listening.

"Well?"

"You're trying to lay it on Martha Hammer, aren't you? You may be right. What do you want me to do?"

"Sydney gone yet?"

"Yeah, I took her out to the airport this morning."

"You think you could get her back here? With Martha? For whatever reason?"

"Maybe. What are your sneaky plans, Riordan-san? I bow to your celestial wisdom."

"Don't give me the Charlie Chan bit, partner. One, I think that Victoria Small can identify Martha as one who visited Therese shortly before her death. . . . "

"We know that. Martha told you she did."

187

"Ah, yes but Victoria can place her at Therese's house at just about the time the murder was committed. And, we have to get a fingerprint from Martha."

"Shit, Riordan! You have lost your mind. It's been comin' but now it's here. How's Victoria's ID of Martha going to change anything? And so her fingerprints were there. So were yours. So were mine."

"Maybe, just maybe, it can push her into a confession. There just ain't any other way."

## 45
*This is not a ghost story, friends.*

THAT NIGHT I had my looking-for-the-car dream again. Damn, it almost never varies. I am looking for my battered Mercedes and it just isn't where I left it. Except there was one significant added attraction this time. Wherever I went searching for the car, around a vast parking lot or block after block of a city, I'd see the image of Therese Colbert, alive and walking toward me. Now this was pretty frightening, seeing as how I had never seen the woman alive. But she *looked* alive, if a little pale. Just as I was about to come face to face with her, I woke up.

I looked at the digital clock at my bedside. Three o'clock. The numerals are illuminated and I can make them out from my bed by opening my left eye. Since it was still dark I concluded, in my infinite wisdom, that it was not three in the afternoon. Why is this old woman haunting me? I thought. I sat up on the edge of the bed and was suddenly wide awake. This is not a ghost story, friends. Ghosts are for spirit medi-

189

ums and Henry James, a writer of dense and truly spooky prose.

No, I was really haunting myself. The woman had intruded on my recurrent dream because I was really angry at myself for having taken so long to run down her killer.

I went into my kitchen and broke open a package of teriyaki turkey jerky which I ate with a handful of fat-free crackers. The stuff immediately created such a flow of stomach acid that I regretted eating the food five minutes after I finished it.

It is hard for me to get used to this house. For years I had to clomp down a narrow staircase to get to the kitchen. Now everything is on the same level, and I'm just getting oriented. When I wake up, it takes thirty or forty seconds to realize where I am. Now I have to think about things I used to do automatically.

I padded back to the bedroom and lay down. I guess sleep crept up on me unexpectedly, because the next time I woke it was broad daylight and the phone was ringing. The taste in my mouth told me that I shouldn't have eaten the jerky, but the ringing of the phone was insistent.

"Riordan, are you just getting out of bed? It's nine o'clock. I've just made a call to Sydney. The deed is done. The die is cast. Who said that? Julius Caesar? Or Lucky Luciano?"

"Reiko, I do not know what the hell you are talking about. Please, dear, my head is foggy. I was up in the middle of the night."

"Sydney and Martha," she said, "are coming down here tomorrow. I gave them a sad little tale of woe, about an attorney who was trying to cheat them, about Sterns."

"That's slander, kid. You could be sued. But you know that."

"I don't think it's possible to slander a lawyer. Even if what you say about him isn't true, there's probably something that he *did* do that he doesn't want anybody to know about. Pretty clever, huh?"

"Since they're not coming until tomorrow, why did you think it was necessary to call me this morning."

"Woke you up, didn't I? Get cleaned up and get the hell down to the office. We do have other things to do, you know."

She was right. The day-to-day crap that kept the wheels turning had to be done. Now and then I longed for the old days of guys like Sam Spade and Philip Marlowe who kept a booze supply in a bottom desk drawer, and who could kick back and drift into an alcoholic haze now and then. Me, I had to live up to the code. I had to stay sober one day at a time. And sober meant that the facts of life were always crystal clear.

On my way to the office I stopped by to see Armand Colbert, who started this whole mess by hiring me. He was sitting in the sun in the patio of his restaurant, sorting out bills and paying some of them.

"How's the food business, Armand?" I asked.

Without looking up, he replied, "Not so good. The nineties have been not so good. Fewer people coming into town. Fewer people willing to pay the price for good meals. They expect prices like McDonald's and food like mine. Nobody has any taste anymore."

"Have you ever eaten at McDonald's? People only *think* it's cheap. It's like those discount houses all over the place now. You get some things cheap and then they stick it to you on other stuff."

Armand was indignant. "No! I have never eaten at McDonald's. Nor Wendy's, nor Carl's Junior. I have had no reason to eat at those places. Riordan, I have operated four successful restaurants. Can you *see* me eating a Big Mac?" He shuddered.

As as matter of fact, I couldn't imagine it. But I hadn't come to Armand's restaurant to discuss gourmet food.

"Since you are no longer paying me, I have no obligation to tell you this, but I must. Reiko and I think we know who killed your aunt. I thought you might like to hear about it. Since you paid me to go to Miami and find out about her."

That got his attention. "What do you know, Pat? Tell me. I'll buy you lunch. I'd give you a bottle of wine, but I know you don't drink."

The offer wasn't much but it was too much to pass up.

"Include Reiko and those two ladies from Miami and it's a deal."

"Those two strange women who flew all the way out here to do nothing to enlighten me? Why them?"

"Maybelle and Victoria have perhaps given me the last nail for the coffin. That is, I think they have. I'll be better able to tell you after tomorrow. But I can tell you this with some confidence. The killer was a woman. One of two. I don't know yet which one."

# 46
## *It was about what I had expected.*

W̲HEN MARTHA and Sydney arrived at my office at eleven the following morning, I decided to take them to lunch in the patio of the General Store. It's just a block from Armand's place, but I didn't want him in on this conference.

It was a gorgeous Carmel day, sunny and bright with just a touch of breeze from the ocean to cool things off. As I sat across the table from my two guests I was again struck by the physical differences between mother and daughter. Sydney was, well, almost what you'd call petite. Martha was a big woman, broad-shouldered, a bit threatening just sitting there. Not too much of a gene-exchange there.

Sydney ordered quiche. That was about right for her. Martha ordered a massive plate of pasta. "It figures," I thought. Reiko, sitting next to me close enough to dig her sharp little elbow in my ribs if she disapproved of anything I said, had the Chinese chicken salad. I think I had a turkey sandwich; I had my mind on other matters and the menu was just a piece of paper with words on it.

As I ate my sandwich, I thought about how I would open the subject with the ladies. The sandwich must have been good; I ate it all. We had coffee and the two guests looked at me expectantly. There was a considerable period of silence.

"Ladies, I have a confession to make. I didn't really invite you here to reveal the dark dealings of Elliott Sterns. That was Reiko's idea. Pure fiction. But I have been having a difficult time reconciling some things that you both have told me during the course of the investigation of Therese Colbert's death."

Both women stiffened and the chill was not from a breeze off Carmel Bay.

"This is unforgivable, Riordan. You have your assistant invite us here for a specific reason that turns out to be a lie. Sydney and I have come some distance because we thought it would be in our interest, and now we find it's all a fiction. What are you doing? Are you accusing one of us of murdering Therese?"

"Firstly, Reiko is my partner, not my assistant. And I'm sorry about the fiction. However, I'm not going to kneel and beg forgiveness. The fact of the matter is that both of you visited Therese shortly before Reiko and I discovered her body. And I have a notion that one of you is not telling the truth about what happened during those visits."

Sydney had not said a word after lunch. She sat and stared at me. Her mouth worked as if she wanted to speak but nothing came out. Her face was a kind of mask. It was a pretty face, but at that moment of that day it looked very like the theatrical mask of Tragedy, corners of the mouth turned down, brow furrowed, eyes, beautiful blue eyes, looking at me as if I had just suggested that the sky was falling. But no Chicken Little, I.

We were beginning to attract a bit of attention from other customers. An elderly couple dressed in summer wear that must have been fashionable in some small midwestern town moved from the table adjacent to ours to a spot in a far corner. A waitress (I still refuse to say "waitperson") who had approached us with a glass coffee pot inched away when she saw the look on Martha's face.

Sydney, shaken, began to speak: "Everything I told you was the truth. My girl friend left Orlando to visit her family in Ocala. I went to Miami to see my grandmother. Our meeting was just as I described it. She had no feeling for me, and I made no demands of her. Period. Mother?"

It was Martha's turn. "I admit that I visited Therese. I admit that we argued. I may have threatened her with legal action. But I did not kill her."

It was about what I had expected. Denials from both women. Par for the course.

I addressed both of them. "What if I told you that your fingerprints were found in Therese's house? And that a neighbor woman saw you, Martha, enter the place at just about the time the coroner has fixed as the approximate time of death."

"Of course our fingerprints were there, I'm sure. We both admit to having been there." Martha was very cool.

I continued: "Let me take it a step further. Suppose the fingerprints of one of you were found on what is believed to be the murder weapon? How would you explain that?"

Martha's face didn't change expression, but a pallor began to appear in her cheeks and her brow. "That simply could not be, Riordan. The knife was wiped clean."

She stopped suddenly, aware that she had gone just a sentence too far. Nobody at the table said a word for at least a full minute. The pain from Reiko's elbow in my ribs was a pain of approval, I think.

The Forge in the Forest, which is what the patio of the General Store is called, used to be a real forge. For many years, a guy made wrought iron gadgets in this very spot. Now it's full of lush greenery and bright flowers. The day, as I have said, was mild and bright. A perfect day in a perfect setting.

At long last, Martha spoke: "Sydney, you'd best drive me home. I need to speak to my attorney. We have wasted enough of our time here."

Sydney helped her mother from the bench on which she sat in this lovely garden restaurant. She gave an agonized glance at Reiko and then steadied the older woman as she left.

Reiko was elated and sad at the same time. I know it's hard to do, but she can do some impossible things.

"It *was* Martha. I've got mixed emotions, Riordan."

"I can see that, partner. Tell me about 'em."

"It's Sydney. She's so nice. So sweet. So loyal to her mother. Martha is an unmitigated bitch, but Sydney still loves her, you see. That's got to get to you."

"Yeah, honey, Sydney is a nice little girl. But Mama is a killer. All I can feel is relief."

Reiko shook her head. I paid the check with a credit card, trusting that I was still under my limit. The card had been my late wife's and the bank behind it was glad to change it into my name when she died. That's the only way I could qualify before I got sober in San Francisco. If the bank guys could have seen me then they would have pulled the thing in a blink.

I didn't feel much like celebrating the end of this case. I got a trip to Miami out of it, a week in Florida. Reiko had her purse snatched and two tourists from Europe were murdered on the street while we were there. It was hot and muggy and damned uncomfortable. The rest of the action involved with the murder of Therese Colbert didn't earn me a goddam dime. So there was no feeling of triumph when Martha Hammer gave herself away over coffee after lunch in a nice Carmel restaurant. Just a sort of grim satisfaction.

Reiko and I walked down Fifth to the restaurant Armand lovingly calls Casanova. The lunch crowd was in high gear so we had to talk to him on the street.

"Well, I guess I should thank you, Patrick. I do not begrudge the young woman her just inheritance. I'm glad it

was not she who murdered my aunt. But I am sad that
Therese is dead, and I am angry at the other woman who
killed her. Too bad, too bad." He frowned and looked at the
sidewalk. "I suppose this means that you will be claiming that
free lunch I promised you. With the two charming ladies from
Florida. Could you possibly make it a weekday? I'm just
beginning to get a healthy weekend business."

"Sure, pal. Let's make it Monday or Tuesday. And Armand,
don't make us order the special. It's got to be a la carte and
your treat, right?"

Reluctantly, he agreed. I brought Sally along without telling
him, but he didn't seem to notice. Maybelle, Victoria, Reiko,
Sally and I feasted royally on Armand's best cuisine washed
down with his best wine. Except for me, of course. The wine,
I mean. There's this little warning buzzer in my brain that
goes off when I'm at a meal like this. A couple of glasses of
wine and I might be up, up and away, like a beautiful balloon.
That I don't need.

DiSalvo, the lawyer, got Martha to turn herself in and be
extradited to Florida. Working with Sterns, he got her to
make a plea bargain to manslaughter, which I thought was a
slick bit of work. But, after all, Martha had done what she
did in a passionate rage, I guess, and she wasn't going to be a
public menace. She got a prison term with possibility of
parole in five years. I have a notion that she is doing some
kind of clean work in an office or the library, and has a TV in
her cell.

Sydney and Reiko are still good friends. They talk on the
phone about once a week and exchange visits. It's funny,
though, that Reiko is at least ten years older than Sydney. But
then Reiko doesn't seem to age at all. She hasn't grown an
inch or gained a pound since the first time I saw her through
the mists of a nasty hangover in my old San Francisco office
years ago.

Sally didn't agree to marry me. Damn, I though she was on
the verge when she saw my house. But she said no, she just

wasn't ready. I'm not sure I want to marry Sally now. I'm getting used to the house on Santa Fe street. It's still close to town and it's bright and airy and in a quiet neighborhood.

Maybe I'll just kick back and enjoy life here. Maybe I had one good marriage, and one is about all a guy can expect.

Especially a guy who is getting pretty gray and just a bit overweight.

Especially a guy who will never be a World Class Private Investigator.

Maybe I could write murder mysteries for a living. It ought to be easy.

## ABOUT THE AUTHOR

Roy Gilligan is a man of indeterminate age, born seventeen blocks south of the Mason-Dixon Line in Covington, Kentucky, a city noteworthy as the birthplace of Durward Kirby and Una Merkel. He graduated from the University of Cincinnati quite a while ago, and was gainfully employed for a considerable period of time in the communications media before deciding to teach English in a California public high school. He has had one wife and one daughter, five dogs (all now deceased), and is proud of two bright and beautiful grandchildren. He is happy to be living in Carmel, California, about two miles as the crow flies from the eighteenth green at Pebble Beach. He is equally happy that he never took up golf, thereby saving an enormous amount of money in greens fees.

IF YOU LIKED THIS BOOK . . .

The Pat Riordan–Reiko Masuda series began with *Chinese Restaurants Never Serve Breakfast* in 1986. Since then, Brendan Books has published *Live Oaks Also Die, Poets Never Kill, Happiness is Often Deadly,* and *Playing God . . . and other games.* All these titles are available from

Brendan Books
P.O. Box 221143
Carmel, California 93922

If you'd like to have one or another, send $8.95 plus $1.50 for postage and handling to the above address. California residents add appropriate sales tax.

These books are available through local bookstores that use R.R. Bowker Company's *Books In Print* catalog system. Bookstore discount available through publisher.

Brendan Books are distributed to the trade by Capra Press.